Frances Eastwood

Marcella: The fearless Christian maiden

A tale of the early church

Frances Eastwood

Marcella: The fearless Christian maiden
A tale of the early church

ISBN/EAN: 9783741189180

Manufactured in Europe, USA, Canada, Australia, Japa

Cover: Foto ©Andreas Hilbeck / pixelio.de

Manufactured and distributed by brebook publishing software
(www.brebook.com)

Frances Eastwood

Marcella: The fearless Christian maiden

MARCELLA:

THE FEARLESS CHRISTIAN MAIDEN.

A TALE OF THE EARLY CHURCH.

BY

FRANCES EASTWOOD.

"THE NOBLE ARMY OF MARTYRS PRAISE THEE."

NEW YORK:

DODD & MEAD, PUBLISHERS,

Successors to M. W. Dodd,

No. 762 BROADWAY.

No. 762 Broadway.

STEREOTYPED BY
DENNIS BRO'S & THORNE,
AUBURN, N. Y.

TO THE MEMORY OF

MY FRIEND,

WHO, WHEN THIS WORK WAS BEGUN,

INCITED ME BY HER INTELLIGENT SYMPATHY;

BUT TO WHOM, ERE IT WAS FINISHED,

WAS REVEALED THE FULL GLORY

OF

ETERNAL LIFE.

PREFACE.

WE, to whom the doctrine of immortality has been familiar from childhood, and for whom death has always been robbed of its worst terrors by revelations of the Gospel, can scarcely comprehend the emotions of those to whom it was suddenly revealed in mature life. The early Christian found many of the doctrines and practices not so very far removed from the philosophy of the ancient sages, but not even Plato had been able to dispel for the shrinking soul the anticipated horrors of annihilation.

As justification by faith may be said to be the key which opened to the priest-ridden nations of the middle ages the door of the Reformation, so the doctrine of the immortality of the soul, with its revelation of a glorious heaven awaiting those faithful to the end, was that grand point in Christianity which appealed most strongly to the feelings of the pagan, and answered most perfectly the cravings of his awakened spirit. It was this that endued them with that fortitude under the most fearful tortures which was so incomprehensible to their enemies, and the sight of which not unfrequently caused the executioners to throw aside their instruments of cruelty to place themselves in the ranks of their victims.

It is my earnest wish that this simple story may arouse in the reader's mind a deeper sense of the riches of God's love in bringing immortality to light through His Son, and revealing to us the two most glorious truths which ever dawned to enlighten a sin-blinded world—Jesus and the Resurrection.   FRANCES EASTWOOD.

CONTENTS.

CONTENTS.

MARCELLA OF ROME.

CHAPTER I.

The End of the Voyage.

THE afternoon sun was shining with a splendor unusual even over that sunniest of all seas—the blue Mediterranean. And very blue those waters were; so calm as to reflect every curve of the Grecian galley floating on their bosom, so transparent that the idle sailors on the vessel's prow could watch the startled fishes fathoms below, as they darted hither and thither, frightened by the measured dip of the long oars into their retreats. Not a breath of air was stirring. The purple sails of the ship hung in heavy masses against the gayly-painted masts; the glassy surface of the deep was unbroken save by the slowly widening circles made at each plash of the oars, and the gentle ripples under the sharp, high prow, as it cut its way slowly through the water. Even within the ship all seemed hushed and dreamy. The sailors were either lying asleep on the shady side of the deck, or were leaning over the bulwarks gazing at the sea, and at the long line of blue, hazy coast that every moment was bringing them nearer. The very galley slaves had hushed the monotonous chant with which they were accustomed to accompany their weary labors to a tune so low that it seemed to chime in with the stillness rather than break it.

At the extreme forward part of the vessel, on a heap of luxurious cushions, sat, or rather reclined, a youth whose thoughts seemed wandering far away from the surrounding objects. He was a Greek, and a pure blooded and high-born Greek, as one might see from a glance at the rather low, but well-shaped forehead, shaded with curls of thick brown hair, the eyes clear, full, and deep set, the long straight nose, the perfectly cut mouth and chin, and the whole expression of his graceful, but rather effeminate figure. With one hand he was caressing a little dog that lay beside him, with the other he defended his head from the sharp corners of the ship's side, against which he leaned. His thoughts seemed somewhat to trouble him, for every now and then he would knit his brow as if in perplexity, or curl the corners of his mouth into a contemptuous smile.

But at length one frown, deeper and more prolonged than any that had preceded it, was dissipated by a touch from a little soft hand, which, after smoothing out the wrinkles from his forehead, passed gently over his other features until it was caught and imprisoned in one of his. However disagreeable his thoughts may have been, they all vanished in a moment, and left only an amused expression on his face as he regarded the new-comer. He did not, however, offer to move in order to make room on the cushions beside him, but she, after waiting a moment, just pushed the dog aside, and kneeling on one knee gazed with eager curiosity upon the approaching shores.

They were evidently brother and sister. Features and expression were the same in both; but the delicately cut features which made his face too effeminate for manly beauty, were in hers only feminine delicacy, and his air of irresolution and languor became in her more like that timidity and gentleness which form so attractive a part of a young girl's character. Her hair, which was of a deep gold color, was turned back from her forehead, and having been twisted around her head in heavy braids, was fastened with an ivory pin. Her mantle of azure blue, contrasting well with the whiteness of her neck and arms, was fastened at the throat by an enameled clasp representing Psyche playing with Cupid ; and opening at the waist showed an under tunic of fine white woolen stuff, embroidered and confined at the waist by a girdle of blue and gold.

Neither spoke for some time ; at last the dog, starting up, began to lick his mistress' hand and bark joyously. Then the girl broke the silence.

"See! Hylax knows as well as any one that we are near our journey's end. Ah! old fellow, you and I will be glad to have a run together on the firm ground once more, though we have had a lovely voyage since leaving Sicily."

"Are you, then, in such haste to meet all

your unknown relations?" said her brother languidly; "for my part I would rather our prow were turned the other way, and we sailing between the Pillars of Hercules out into that great mysterious sea, than about to encounter the unknown dangers of so many new acquaintances."

"Not entirely new to you, Philip; you knew them when you were in Rome before."

"The older ones, yes; but twelve years make a great difference in people, at least I find it has in you and me. It is more than likely that we shall have quite grown out of each other's recollection, and have to begin our acquaintance all over again; that is, if there is any acquaintance at all."

"Why, Philip, what do you mean? Of course we will know them, and like them some time; Marcella is older than I am, is she not?"

"Older! Yes, I should think so," said the

young Greek with a peculiar smile, "fifty years at least."

"Philip! I wish you would not tease me," said the girl petulantly. "I really want to know something about them all. You told me she was younger than you?"

"Well, yes, inasmuch as she was born the year after me; but one of our old sages says that some persons live more in a year than others in a century, and Marcella certainly belongs to the former class. Counting that way she must be several hundred years old by this time. See! Eudora, those white walls are Ostia; soon we shall be at the gates of the Mistress of the World."

"She was only a wolf's cub till she got civilization from us," replied the girl with a disdainful toss of her head. "But I want to hear more about these cousins; we will see Rome fast enough."

"And the people in it too," replied her

brother dryly; "so I do not wish to prejudice your mind either for or against them, especially as I know little worth telling. There was one older than Marcella, a son, Severus; I know you would have liked him, but he is dead. I think his death must have been a very sad thing for Marcella, for he seemed to be the only one she cared for besides her books of philosophy. There were two others younger who died in infancy. I believe there have been several since."

"And the father?" said Eudora.

"'Of him I knew very little. He was away for some time at the wars, and I believe distinguished himself. The mother is quiet and gentle, one of those people, I fancy, who, although they do much to make everything go smoothly in the household and in society, keep themselves in such dark corners that they never get the credit for it."

"Quite different from our mother then,

Philip; it would take a very dark corner to hide her. I don't see how she ever came to let me come along with you, unless it was because I was such a trouble to her at home, and she thought that perhaps Marcella might inject me with a little of her wisdom. How she would scold now if she saw me in this embroidered robe, that she thinks only ought to see the light on festal days; and without my veil!"

"Are you dressed up in this way in order to impress your unknown friends, the wolf's cubs?" said her brother mischievously, as he watched the girl bending over the vessel's side in order to use the smooth water for a mirror while she clasped and unclasped her mantle, and pulled her tunic into its most becoming folds.

Eudora blushed a little, perhaps her brother had interpreted too well her thoughts; at any rate she stopped her impromptu toilet and began caressing the dog, pointing out to him the objects around, while he, wise fellow looked as if he comprehended her perfectly.

"There is no use in trying to captivate Marcella with the latest Athenian fashions for embroidery and cameoes," continued Philip; "if you could inform her concerning some new system of philosophy, or bring her some hitherto unknown fragment of a Greek tragedy, you might hope to get into her good graces; but as for all the little vanities of woman's daily life, she walks as far above them as yon sun does over these gaudy masts and sails of ours. But now down with your veil, Eudora, here comes the shipmaster."

The maiden veiled herself instantly, according to Greek custom, and sank gracefully back on the cushions as a firm step sounded on the deck, and a cheery voice saluted them.

"Good day, my lady Eudora, art thou wearied yet of the sea and our rough company?"

"Never of the sea!" replied the young girl enthusiastically, "especially when we have such weather. It seems more like floating through the air in the car of Juno, than combating Neptune in his own element."

"Yes, lady, this has been a most successful voyage, thanks to Castor and Pollux; I shall never henceforth sail without their image fastened to the masthead. We will land very soon now, and the distance from Ostia to Rome is not great. It is to Marcus, the vintner, that I am to conduct you, is it not?"

"That is our destination," replied the young man carelessly; "but for my part, good Archippus, I would that we were sailing out beyond the Pillars of Hercules rather than up this peaceful Tiber."

"Say you so?" said the shipmaster, shrugging his shoulders, "that would be tempting the gods rather too far. I doubt if even the twin deities would avail to protect us among the dangers of those unknown seas, on the very borders of the earth. Why they say the water there boils like a caldron, and the winds blow every way at once. Better thank the fates, young man, that you are going to a place where there is more pleasure and less danger. There are many gay sights in Rome now since the emperor's return. Mock sea-fights in the Naumachiæ, and gladiatorial combats in all the forii. Marcus, it is true, does not dwell in the city, but quite close at hand, and you can come in any day you like. But do you know that he and his family are said to have joined this new and rather disreputable sect called Christians? Their idea is to dethrone all the gods, and worship a man whom the governor of Galilee, a paltry province in Syria, crucified for trying to make himself king."

Philip looked vexed, and uttered an expression of disgust and impatience.

"Ay, ay, I know what they are; they are increasing all over Greece, and I have heard that Rome is full of them. But if it proves to be really as you say, Archippus, we shall seek the protection of other friends in the city, or return with you in your vessel to Athens; respect at least for antiquity would keep us from residing with those who refuse to honor the gods of our ancestors; besides, they must have sunk by such an act too far in the scale of society to be either agreeable or useful acquaintances. When do you return?"

"Not for two months; but do not be alarmed, it may be only a false report, for whenever any one pretends to be particularly moral, they call him a Christian; or they may have turned back again. Time will decide. We will anchor soon, and then, ho! for Rome!"

"How very provoking!" exclaimed Eudora,

as Archippus left them; "but you do not think that Marcella will have given herself up to this madness, do you?"

"No," said Philip meditatively, "it generally seems to take hold only of the unlearned; and she is certainly very wise, from all I have heard, and may have risen above it. Most of the Christians at Rome are the Jossi and common laborers. Pah! to think of worshiping a crucified man!"

"But he did some miracles, and very wonderful ones too, Philip."

"When did you hear that?" said Philip, surprised.

"Old Armenna, my nurse's mother, says that when she was a child she saw one of the disciples of this man, the last one left of twelve. His name was John, and he was very old, but so good and gentle and beautiful; and he told many things that Jesus of Nazareth had done—opening the eyes of the blind, healing the sick, and even raising the dead to life."

"You should not listen to Armenna, Eudora, she is old; it does not do to believe everything that old persons say; they forget some things, and invent others to fill up their stories. But she is not a Christian, is she?"

"No, but she says she wishes she was one, for they have no fear of anything, not even of death, for they believe they cannot die."

"Each one finds himself mistaken once in his life, then. But we will not talk of such a dreadful thing while we are young and everything is so bright about us. See, Eudora, they are preparing to anchor!"

It was indeed so. The low chant of the galley slaves changed to shouts of joy as they pulled in the long dripping oars, and dropped them with one loud clang into their places. Some of the mariners drew down and secured the sails. Where all had appeared so very

quiet an hour ago, all was now life and motion. Soon the anchors were dropped from
prow and stern, the vessel swung round, tug-
·ging at her cables, then settled herself with
some creaking timbers, and the last ripples
died away from her sides. The voyage was
over.

CHAPTER II.

Marcella.

IT had been a bustling, exciting day in Rome. The emperor had attended an unusually magnificent gladiatorial show in the Colosseum, and now that he and his court were returning home, the streets were filled with elegant chariots and splendidly dressed nobles. The ponderous vehicles, driven at headlong speed, thundered over the stone pavement of the Via Sacra, and the clouds of dust thus raised admitted only an occasional glimpse of glittering armor, brilliant colored robes, prancing Egyptian and Arabian horses, and streaming banners which had been borne in triumph over almost every known part of the world.

2

It must have been a noble sight to any one standing on the Capitoline Hill, or to a spectator of the games, who, lingering on the highest tier of the Colosseum, gazed down and along the whole length of the sacred street, the great thoroughfare of the Mistress of the World, lined with the palaces and pleasure grounds of those who had been the world's conquerors. A noble sight it must have been from many points, and all Rome seemed to have come out to gaze upon it. The windows of the many-storied houses were crammed with women and children, each in her gayest attire. The narrow, tortuous alleys, which opened out of the principal streets, were choked with a surging, tumultuous crowd that fought amongst themselves for every little elevation which promised a better view, and shouted out their delight as some favorite senator or general passed by. The shops, too, were doing a thriving business. All along the Via Tuscus, ever famous for its wine-shops, were groups of men making their way to and from their favorite places of entertainment, thirsty after the choking dust, and hoarse from their vociferous cheering.

Rome enjoyed such days; and now that the emperor had returned a victor from so many conflicts in the east and north, it seemed likely they would become quite frequent. He had brought with him prisoners enough to furnish gladiatorial shows for many months, besides wild beasts; and there were rumors of a grand mock combat to come off in the Campus Martius between the captives of different nations, in which there would be enough blood spilt to satisfy even that blood-loving city. No wonder Rome was in a tumult of happiness; at the very zenith of her power, riches pouring in on every side, monarchs of countries that were old when Remus

leaped in derision over his brother's mud
walls, languishing in her prisons, or paying
her humiliating tribute—everything to hope
for, nothing to fear—who had a right like her
to be intoxicated with gladness?

But far away from the Via Sacra, with its
palaces and tumult—far away from the Colosseum, reeking with the blood of victims sacrificed to gratify a barbarous fondness for witnessing human suffering, beyond the Servian
wall that the city had long outgrown, in one
of the streets leading out into the Campagna,
there was a contrast very refreshing to the
wearied eye and ear.   There were a few
passers-by, but no chariots.   Instead of the
dust there was a delicate perfume of gardens
and vineyards.   Instead of the many-storied
palaces, there were long reaches of low, irreg-
ular wall, covered with vines and overhung
with trees.   Instead of the hoarse shouts of
the multitude, there were the sounds of some

children at play, and a maiden singing at her latticed window.

One of the gardens which lined this pleasant street belonged to a house which stood in the middle of it, and was altogether very plain and unpretending, although it had an air of taste and comfort, and even of elegance, about it. There were no marble columns and statues, or bronze vases, or sculptured fountains; but some climbing vines had been gracefully trained over the entrance, the flower beds were well weeded and in full beauty, and the walks neatly kept. There was a vineyard behind, and some fruit and shade trees quite overshadowing the house.

Under one of these trees a table was set and a meal in progress. The beams of the setting sun flickering through the leaves as they were moved hither and thither by the breeze, lighted now on the simple dishes decked with leaves and flowers, now on the faces of the company.

At one end, leaning against the trunk of the tree, sat the father of the family, a hardy, weather-beaten soldier, who having fought many battles in Gaul, Britain, and Germany, and lost two fingers from his right hand, thus unfitting him for further duty, had returned to cultivate his little plot of land, and enjoy the rest of his days with his family. That family was gathered all around him now, and he seemed both fond and proud of it. His wife sat opposite to him with a baby in her arms, trying to still its crowings so that the father's voice might be heard above the tumult which it was assisting its two little brothers to make. In the places of honor, on the right and left of the host, sat the two young Greeks—Eudora gay and chattering, Philip silent, with an expression of doubt mingled with wonder and scorn, on his face; for he felt with regard to that part of the family which he had already seen, there remained little doubt but that they had embraced the doctrine of the despised Nazarene. At the beginning of the repast the father had risen, and all stood with bowed heads, while he uttered a thanksgiving that was not addressed to Jupiter, or any other of the residents on Mount Olympus, and which was closed with the name of the crucified pretender; and now a few careless words from Eudora, more than confirmed his suspicions.

The little ones seemed to have taken a great fancy to her bright face and lively talk, and were offering to show her all kinds of pretty things on the morrow.

"There is one thing that I wish very much you would show me. I suppose we ought to offer some sacrifice to Castor and Pollux for our prosperous voyage, and you can show us the way to their temple."

The boy's eyes opened wide with astonishment, and it was a moment before he answered.

"We do not go to temples nor do sacrifice,
cousin; you must thank *God* for bringing you
in safety over the seas; Castor and Pollux
had nothing to do with it."

"How now!" exclaimed Eudora, the color
rising in her face, partly from amusement,
partly from vexation. "It seems to me you
are rather young to be dethroning the divinities in such an off-hand fashion. Cannot
you be content to worship your God, and let
me worship mine?"

"There cannot be two gods," said the boy
stoutly. "Yours are nothing at all; mine
made you and me and all the world, and
takes care of us; he gave us our supper
to-night; Castor and Pollux cannot do that!"

"No; we thank Ceres for corn, and Bacchus for the fruit of the vine. But tell me,

my little philosopher, how it is that your God brought me safe over the seas when I never cared a bit for him? I should have thought he would have let us alone, or rather have upset our vessel, and tumbled us all to the bottom of the sea, if he really cared anything about whether we served him or not, for I have never so much as offered him a garland in my whole life, and don't much think I ever shall."

The boy was undismayed by this avowal of opinions so at variance with those he had been taught. He only stood a moment or two in deep thought; then, starting up, laid a grasp, rather rougher than was good for the delicate material on her tunic, climbed upon her knee, and laid his head upon her shoulder.

"I'll tell you why God has taken care of you so long, though you didn't love him, and why he wouldn't let you be drowned. He wanted you to come here and learn to be a

2*

Christian, and love Jesus Christ, and live for his honor, and die for the truth! *That's* why he didn't let you drown, cousin Eudora, and I'm so glad he didn't."

The last words ended in a sob, and Eudora felt the child's hot tears on her neck as she looked up, somewhat confounded at this turn of affairs, into the father's face.

Marcus pitied her confusion, and, stooping, loosened the little one's grasp, and took him into his own arms, saying, in a kind tone:

"I believe with my little son, Eudora, that God has sent you here to us for a wise and good purpose of his own; and it has been my earnest prayer to him since I first heard of your coming to Rome that to you and your brother, before you quit my roof, all the gods and goddesses in whom you have trusted from your childhood may seem but as creatures of a dream, and the one great reality of life be Jesus and the resurrection!"

Eudora felt sadly bewildered. Her jest had ended in very sober earnest. She did not half understand what Marcus meant, only that he thought she was going to turn Christian, and how annoyed Philip would be! She had no answer, and turned to her brother for aid; but he had slipped away. He did not like dissensions, and he generally contrived to slip out of anything that was troublesome or disagreeable to him; so finding herself alone, she only said: "I suppose you mean kindly, thank you," and stooped down to caress Hylax, and feed him with what remained on her plate.

The mother had gone to lay her child in the cradle but now returned.

"It is growing late, Marcus," she said a little anxiously, "and Marcella has not returned, and the city is so tumultuous to-day; what can have detained her?"

"The Lady Paulina is not wont to keep her late," replied the father cheerily; "she may

have been detained by the crowd in the Via
Sacra."

"There she comes!" shouted the little one
from his high post of observation on his
father's shoulder. "Put me down quick,
father; I must have her first kiss!"

It took but a moment for the child to
struggle out of his father's arms, and then
he ran at full speed down the garden walk
shouting: "'Cella's come home! 'Cella's come,
and I'm so glad! Cousin Philip, cousin Eudora, come see Marcella!"

Eudora pushed the dog away, and rose
eagerly, with a merry word of reproach on
her lips for Marcella, for having been away
when they arrived; but she forgot it entirely,
and stood quite abashed at her own presump-
tion, as she looked down the path at the figures advancing toward her. The little one
was the image of quiet, beaming happiness,
as he trotted along at his sister's side; his

still tear-stained face peeping out from the folds of her dress, which he had clutched in both hands, as if afraid she might try to escape from him.

She was tall and slender, yet not slightly built; the symmetry of her form fully shown by her plain, scanty, and almost coarse dress. She could not be called pretty or attractive; she was more—she was grandly beautiful. From the bands of jet-black hair, braided in a massive cope, and twisted downwise around her head, to the gently swelling curves of her neck and bosom, there was not a line or a tint but was faultless. Her face was a perfect oval, her complexion that dark, clear, transparent shade, which is only found beneath Italian skies. Her cheeks were flushed a little from exercise, her nose slightly aquiline, with delicately-cut nostrils; the mouth small, and expressive of exquisite sweetness, mingled with quiet firmness. Her eyes were large, deep set, and heavily fringed. It was like looking into a deep, clear well to gaze into their depths. Above them stretched the straight penciled line of brow, showing in its full perfection the smooth, broad, perfectly developed forehead. The expression in those eyes was clear, intellectual, penetrating; but, more than all, it was a look of perfect purity, as if no sinful thought had ever called upon them for revelation or concealment; as if no sinful deed had ever passed before them to cause them to drop with shame. There was no dreaminess in their look, but earnestness, fearlessness, intellectual vigor, power of mind and will. It was a face to startle and awe the stranger at the first glance, until she spoke; and then the exquisite music of her voice made you only realize the wonderful depths of her strong, wise love, and long to throw yourself upon it, and be at rest.

Perhaps some such thoughts passed through

Eudora's mind, as she stood entranced at the vision so unexpectedly presented to her, for her cheeks became many shades more crimson and her eyelids drooped with a timidity quite foreign to her naturally careless, thoughtless spirit, as her hand was taken in both of Marcella's, and a warm kiss was imprinted on her brow. She answered the greeting in a low, frightened tone, and wondered to herself at the involuntary sigh of relief which she gave when Marcella turned away, and she ceased to feel those eyes upon her.

But where was Philip all this time? Walking among the vines in no very agreeable state of mind. Of all horrible things to be roused from his dreamy apathy, and have his indolent visions broken in upon by rude and impertinent practical thoughts, was what he most dreaded. He had no objection to lying stretched out on his cushions, following, with all a Greek's keenness of thought, the intrica-

cies of some metaphysical theory; but when
it came to any discussion which was likely to
shock his fastidious taste and his old-estab-
lished ideas, and to demand imperiously an
exercise of the judgment to decide and the
will to act, he shrank from it as from a pes-
tilence.   He knew enough of Christianity
to know that it was aggressive in its nature,
that it would shock his prejudices, and demand an appeal to his reason.   Not that he
feared being converted to it, such a thought
never entered his brain; but he would be
forced to decide against it, and maintain his
opinions by argument, and he hated to decide anything, and was too indolent to argue.
And here he had come in contact with it the
first thing, the very children would be fling-
ing the hated subject in his face; if Marcella
were as bad, he would not stay another day;
he hated Rome altogether.   He was leaning
against a tree, kicking away some dead leaves,

thus making such a rustling that he did not hear a soft foot-fall behind him, until a hand was laid on his shoulder, and a voice behind him said :

"Welcome to Rome once more, cousin Philip !"

He turned hastily, and to a degree, although not so greatly as in his sister's case, her beauty took him by storm. He had left her a beautiful girl, he found her a beautiful woman ; still there was much of the old familiar look, and after a moment's hesitation, he felt quite at ease.

"Ah ! Marcella, it seems like old times to see you again, and in this garden : the rest are all strange to me ; but even you have altered a great deal."

"Have I ?" said Marcella quietly ; "yes I believe I have ; one ought to alter a great deal in ten years, and you have too. But why are you here all alone ?"

"Ah! you see," said Philip, a little ashamed, "it is the old way with me; when I don't want to answer an argument, I run away from it. But tell me, Marcella, *you* surely are not carried away like the rest with this wild notion—this Christianity!"

For an answer the girl only lifted her eyes and fixed them full upon his face with an expression of mingled compassion and sorrow; and yet there was something of exultant joy in her low, sweet tone, when she spoke at last:

"I am a Christian, Philip, for life, for death, and for eternity!"

At first the young Greek only looked at her in amazement, but then exclaimed with vexation:

"Do you mean to tell me that all your philosophy has not prevailed against the idle tales of Galilean fishermen? As for these common people and children who have no reason, and believe anything, it is not so hard to imagine it, but that *you*, learned in all the wisdom of our famous Greeks, familiar with the sublime utterances of Plato and Socrates —how *you* can be led away thus, passes my comprehension!"

Those deep, dark eyes were full of faith, humility, and perfect peace, as he gazed into them awaiting her answer; but the corners of her mouth were trembling a little, and many thoughts seemed struggling for expression.

"Philip," she said at last, very solemnly, "God grant that the time may come when you too may see that the only true philosophy is to be found in the teachings of Jesus of Nazareth; that these poor fishermen have attained to heights which all the wisdom of Greece never imagined; that they have placed within the reach of the weakest, as well as the most powerful intellect, as blessed *facts*, aspirations, and desires which even those master minds could only vaguely theorize upon and long for. Socrates and Plato could only deduce from nature the hope of a future life; Christ has in himself brought life and immortality to light. Christianity is living, breathing, acting philosophy; it is the substance instead of the shadow, the reality instead of the type, the full and glorious noonday, as compared with the first gray, uncertain streaks of the dawning!"

Marcella's voice sank into a whisper of almost breathless eagerness as she uttered the last words, her cheeks glowing with enthusiasm, her eyes brimming with tears. Philip stood before her abashed, confounded. He had no answer ready. This was no argument to be assaulted by sophistry—it was simply an assertion so stupendous that it could not be mocked, slighted or carelessly denied. He was not sorry for the interruption of Eudora's voice calling him, and only saying, "We are coming!" he hastened down the path, thinking Marcella was following him, and it was not till he stood in the porch that he found she had not done so.

She had only waited for him to disappear behind a turn in the walk before she turned in an opposite direction, further into the leafy recesses of the garden. There, in the most retired portion of it, yet near enough to the wall to be but a few steps from a little gate half concealed by vines, stood a small low building, so concealed also by trees and vines that one not searching for it might have passed it unseen. It was roughly built from the ruins of some ruined temple, for some of the stones still bore the half-effaced symbols of Bacchus and other heathen divinities. The door was of wood, but moved on massive bronze hinges that had once supported a portal four or five times its size. Within, the floor was only earth, beaten hard, except at one end, where it was raised a step, and covered with some old tiles. At this end there was a small window opening toward the east, and beneath it a table. On the right of this table stood a chair and footstool, on the left a stone seat. Opposite against the wall were a few seats, and at one side a font. There was no ornament anywhere except a rudely carved dove with an olive branch over the window, and the monogram " I. H. S." on the front of the table. The room might, perhaps, hold twenty persons, not more. The air was damp and chilly; a bat disturbed by the opening door flew in circles around Marcella's head before it settled again amid the invisible rafters; the gathering twilight only left visible the small opening, with the little space of starlight which it framed in, and the ghost-like whiteness of the font.

A little later the moon peeped in and shot

one glorious beam straight across the chapel
from window to door, illuminating the beautiful face of the Roman maiden as she knelt on
the step, her head slightly bent, her eyes
dewy with tears. Her gaze was fixed on the
sky, but seemed to pierce beyond it into the
mysteries it veiled. Her expression of rapt
communion was sublime in its purity and
holiness. Thus in the solitude and sacred-
ness of this rude little secret Christian church,
this young girl held converse with her heavenly Father, and received day by day strength
needed for her burden. Nor was this burden
light. In every lane or alley, wherever there
were sick to nurse or the troubled to soothe,
the dying to aid or the mourner to comfort,
the erring to advise or the penitent to console,
the thoughtless to warn or the timid to cheer,
there she walked, sunshine in her loving smile,
music in her gentle voice; thus daily, in that
great capital of the world, filled with luxury

and misery, splendor and suffering, wrong and violence, fearing none, loving and blessing all, went to and fro the fearless Christian girl, Marcella of Rome.

CHAPTER III.

Paulina.

IT wanted yet two hours of noon, on the third day after Philip's arrival, when Marcella stopped before the gate of a large house in the Via Sacra, and pulled the silken cord which sounded a bell within. In a moment a slave opened the bronze door, and, evidently recognizing her by the smile that lit up his otherwise sullen-looking face, suffered her to enter without a word. Well might he remember her. She had nursed him through three months of African fever, and, what made a still closer bond between them, had been the first to open to the bondman the freedom of the Gospel. As he conducted her across the court, and under a beautifully sculptured marble archway, he paused a moment, and said, in a low tone:

"The young mistress is very anxious to see you; I was to go in search of you, if you had not come by noon."

"The Lady Paulina is not ill, is she?" asked Marcella hurriedly.

"No; but—pardon me," said Cyril, hesitating and blushing, "but she does not seem to be able to take hold of the comfort, and I—I'm nothing but a poor slave, and couldn't say anything; but you will know, you will tell her just the right thing! You will comfort her!"

"God will comfort her," said Marcella; and without waiting to hear more, she passed on alone into the grand hall or atrium. This was a very large apartment, open to the sky in the centre, beneath which opening was a tank or open cistern of rare Egyptian marble, which received the water from the roof from four dragon-headed spouts, and was, besides, supplied by a fountain in the centre. This fountain was formed by a group of statues. Cupid, standing on the shoulders of three water-nymphs, was pouring water over them from an urn. Vases of flowering plants stood around, some containing vines which were trained upon the pillars supporting the roof. The pavement was of different-colored marbles, set in a mosaic pattern; the walls were frescoed; and the doors, which opened on every side, were of costly wood and bronze. These doors opened into various apartments, furnished with all the magnificence which characterized the palaces of the nobles in that age of luxury and extravagance. But Marcella did not stay to examine all this; it was by no means new to her; she pressed on, and entered a door at the furthest side of the atrium.

The room in which she found herself was not large, but was furnished with a magnificence which even in Rome itself had few parallels. The floor was covered with a thick Persian carpet, over which the foot passed noiselessly. The light was subdued by passing through crimson curtains, but was prevented from being too sombre by the brilliant colors with which the walls were painted. The tables, made of the most costly wood, were covered with little ornaments in gold, silver, ivory, crystal, and precious stones. There were divans or couches covered with rich material; and a mirror of burnished silver, supported by a massive stand of the same metal, stood in one corner. There were also brackets against the wall, and pedestals of bronze and gilt, holding lamps or statuettes. On one of the couches a fair young girl was reclining.

She was beautiful, but of a beauty so very different from that of Marcella that a comparison between them would be impossible.

She was small, delicate, even fragile in her figure; her complexion so pure and transparent that the veins in her temples showed almost painfully. Her features were small, and with no decided expression, except a childlike gentleness and simplicity. Her eyes, soft and brown, had in them the timid, startled, imploring look of the hunted fawn. Her hair, curling in chestnut ringlets, was drawn back behind her ears, and then fell over a golden comb. Her dress was of violet color, embroidered with gold, and clasped by a richly jeweled belt. A chain of gold hung about her neck, and bracelets of gold and gems were upon her slender wrists.

With one of these she was languidly playing, when she was startled by the opening of the door, and in a moment sprang forward with a cry of joy, and flung both her arms around her visitor's neck. Marcella gently disengaged the clasp, but retained both her hands in her own, and looked down with her peculiarly· peaceful smile into the anxious young face.   That smile seemed to give relief even before words came:

"O Marcella! I am so glad you have come! I am so weak, so fearful, and there is no one to comfort me!"

"Nay, Lady Paulina," replied Marcella, kindly but reprovingly, "whom the Lord Jesus and his Comforter cannot comfort is beyond human aid.   You have not lost your trust in him, surely?"

"No—not my belief.   He is my Saviour, there is none other; but I am so weak, so faithless.   I sit here, and doubt and wonder and fear.   If he were only alive, and I could go to him, and lay hold of him, and not let him go until he told me with his own voice that I was forgiven, then I should feel the healing within me; now I do not, all seems dark and black."

"Blessed are they, who, not having seen, believe."

"I know it, I know it all; but I cannot be blessed in anything; I am not worthy of it."

"Who is worthy?" said Marcella soothingly. "There is One whose righteousness covereth all: 'My grace is sufficient for thee.'"

"But you do not know all!" exclaimed Paulina, her eyes filling with tears; "I have denied the faith again. Only yesterday, when Julia and Victoria were here, I helped them weave garlands for the temple of Apollo; and gave them my flowers because they laughed at me, and said I was too dreamy and idle to know a rose from a lily; and then, afterward, my father was scoffing at the Christians, and accusing them of all kinds of crime, and I held my peace."

The last words ended in a sob; and for a moment Marcella was troubled, and hardly knew how to answer. She was herself endowed with such a measure of moral and physical courage that she could hardly sympathize with such an entire want of both. With her, to accept Christianity was to abandon at once and forever every trace of heathenism. Her strength of will and decision of character made even long-established habit and deep-rooted superstition but slight obstacles when once her intellect had convinced her of their sinfulness or absurdity. Her dangers lay in a different path; her battles were fought on different grounds. She could pity; she could hardly sympathize, she could hardly advise. Her delay aroused Paulina's anxiety.

"Oh! do not tell me there is no hope—that he will not forgive!"

"I could not tell you that," replied Marcella gravely, "for it would not be true; but you have sinned grievously. How can we expect him to acknowledge us in that last great day, if we deny him on earth? Shall we fear the mocking of weak men, and not the wrath of an offended God? You must acknowledge him before men, Lady Paulina, before you can have peace; you must let your father know what you are—your father, your friends, all Rome, if need be. I firmly believe that, once openly declared a Christian, you would at least know the worst; and then you would be admitted to the strengthening and comforting sacraments of the Church. It is by the profession of the lips as well as the belief in the heart that salvation is to be obtained."

"But, O Marcella!" cried the girl, shrinking and trembling at the very thought, "you do not know my father; he is so bitter against you—Christians, I mean. You would have shuddered, too, if you had heard his curses and threats; oh! they were fearful. And to have him hurl them at me! Oh! I would, indeed I would; but I cannot."

3*

"You can do all things through Christ strengthening you," replied Marcella hopefully. "Yes, even this seemingly impossible thing will be easy for you, when done for his sake and by his aid. You have not come to the moment of trial yet, and so you do not know the strength which will at that very moment be bestowed upon you. Do you remember how I first taught you to swim in your father's baths—that you would not believe in the resistance of the water until I persuaded you to throw yourself boldly upon it? Then you found how it upbore you."

"Ah! even you never taught me to do anything boldly," replied Paulina sadly, but in a calmer tone. "I would not then have tried if you had not held your arm under, ready to catch me if I sank. Oh! what if Jesus should leave me then, even for a moment! I should perish utterly."

"But that is impossible. He cannot do it."

"*Cannot?*" The word was spoken wonderingly, doubtingly.

"Yes, cannot. Christ can do anything to
comfort the sorrowing, to strengthen the
weak; but he cannot do anything to turn
away the mourner, to hinder the feeble steps
creeping after him, to tear away the trembling
hands clinging to him. Just as a little feeble
babe holds its mother, not by the strength of
its tiny grasp—she cannot forsake it, for her
strong love's sake; she cannot, because she
will not."

Paulina looked up in her friend's face, with
a smile shining through her tears.

"Marcella, I will try. I will this very day!
Only pray for me, that my faith fail not!"

"That is right," replied Marcella cheer-
ingly, caressing the little head that had laid
itself so meekly on her shoulder. "I have
not told you that we have visitors from
Greece."

"Have you?" said the girl, aroused. "Who are they?"

"Cousins, but distant ones, from Ephesus —Philip and Eudora. Philip is my age, and was here once before, when a child. Eudora is a little older than you; seventeen, I should think."

"I would like to know them. Are they Christians?"

"No," replied Marcella sadly; "they are far removed from such things; Eudora by her carelessness and levity, Philip by his philosophy, falsely so-called. But they have only been with us three days, and will probably remain several months with us and other friends, and we will pray that they may not go back again on their long journey without carrying with them the knowledge of Jesus and eternal life."

"That we will, indeed! But, O Marcella! if I could go about as you do, from morning to night, aiding the poor and nursing the sick, instead of idling the whole livelong day! I am so useless in the world!"

"Not quite useless," replied Marcella, smiling. "The coats you made for the widow Susa's children were well bestowed. You should have seen them dance about when they put them on, and the widow's eyes glistened at the sight; and when I put the drachmæ in her hand, and told her they were from you, she bade me tell you that a widow's prayers for her benefactors were pleasant in God's ears, and that hers would arise morning and evening to his throne for your welfare. I had no drachmæ to give; you had, and gave them; I was your messenger. So our Father bestows on us different gifts, but all to be used for his service."

Paulina's face flushed with pleasure, but it clouded again.

"And yet that is nothing. The robe I

fashioned into coats was but an old one.
As for the drachmæ, what are they to me?
What have I ever sacrificed for Him who
left heaven for me?"

Marcella hesitated. She did not know
whether it would be best for that timid,
shrinking girl to know that the step she was
about to take would involve sacrifices she
little dreamed of—sacrifices such as her
friend's tender heart hardly dared realize
for her. She had been considering whether
it would not be best to give her warning of
the consequences which would ensue on her
public acknowledgment of Christianity; but
now these few words made her think that
perhaps these very sacrifices might give her
the strength needed for the struggle. At
any rate she would try.

"Do you think, Lady Paulina, that you
could give up all these luxuries for him if
he asked it?"

The girl gave a glance around the sumptuous apartment.

"Oh! yes, gladly, I think. I am wearied of these lonely rooms. The faces of these foolish gods upon the walls mock at my troubles."

"But cold and hunger and fatigue, Lady Paulina; daily labor with your hands; could you bear all that for Christ?"

"Oh! how can I tell?" replied the poor child piteously. "I would try; but you know I am so weak, so delicate. I could not bear much pain, you know, or work much. He knows that he won't ask it of me; will he?"

"He will ask nothing of you that he does not give you strength for; rest on that. To do, to bear, to suffer for him is a privilege as well as a duty, and brings with it its own peculiar joys; and in the world to come, tears and labor and pain are over forever in the peace of his presence. But, see! the shadow has passed the green pillar; I must be going now."

"Not yet, oh! not yet; not, at least, until you have written something on my tablets to remember while you are gone. Write me a great deal. I will put it in my bosom; and then, when my heart beats so quickly when my father is angry, I will think of them, and take strength!"

Marcella wrote only two texts:

"Fear not, little flock, it is your Father's *good pleasure* to give you the kingdom."

"Commit thy way unto the Lord, and he will bring it to pass."

So she went away with these parting words: "Farewell, dear little trembling lamb, for Jesus' lamb I know you are. Trust in no earthly help, seek no human assistance. Cling close to the kind Shepherd's breast, and he will bring you home safely in his arms."

As Marcella passed among the columns of the atrium, attended by Cyril, the slave who had admitted her, she heard a stir at the outer gate, and, just as she reached the porch, met the owner of the mansion face to face.

Sergius Pollonius was not a pleasant man to meet. His heavy, bloodshot eyes and swollen features, as well as every movement of his bloated, unwieldy figure, told of debauchery and excess; and the deep frown on his brow and the curl of his nostril showed that he did not even possess that careless generosity and good-nature which is often a redeeming virtue in the otherwise vicious. Particularly dark and fierce he looked that day; for he had been only that morning baffled in a favorite scheme of ambition, slighted by the emperor, and dunned by his creditors, any one of which circumstances would have been sufficient to rouse the angry passions of an unprincipled man. His slaves all knew his temper, and stood around cringing and trembling. Marcella, who knew him just as well, alone appeared unmoved. As she passed him on the steps he turned and fixed a gaze upon her of sullen admiration and yet brutal hate.

"Beautiful, by all the gods!" he swore; "but——" Cyril had hastened to close the door behind her and drop the bolt, so that she did not hear the end of the sentence.

"But those Christians have thwarted me this day in the senate, and they shall be crushed!"

There was a little harmless beetle at that moment carrying a grain of corn across the porch toward its nest; the Roman noble made one stride toward it, and with a chuckling laugh ground it into the marble pavement with the heel of his sandal—crushed it as he meant to crush the Christians.

Marcella had passed but a little way down

the Via Sacra when she heard footsteps behind her, and as she paused Cyril came to
her side:

"Pardon," said the slave as he recovered
his breath. "This basket of fruit is for the
children of the widow Susa, and this purse
for herself, or for others as poor; the Lady
Paulina sends them."

The man's message was delivered, but still
he lingered; his dull, expressionless counte-
nance working with some emotion in a most
unaccustomed way. It was not till Marcella
said, "Thanks, Cyril, for your haste, and to
your lady for her gift; have you anything
else that you wish to say?" that his tongue
was loosened.

"Yes. O lady, beware! Tell all the Christians! I am sure there is evil meditated
against them, my lord is so bitter and cruel!"

"But why this sudden hatred?" exclaimed
Marcella; "he was ever indifferent toward

the faith, but never hostile.   What has incensed him against us now?   Surely we have
not harmed him?"

"I may not tell the story right," said poor
Cyril, rubbing his brow in perplexity.   "Cy-
tus, my lord's steward, told me, but I am so
dull, lady.   I think he said that Mutius, the
carpenter in the Via Aureum, would not be
bribed, and by his witness lost him his cause
against the Senator Orinus.   So, lady, pray,
beware!   I must not stay."

"One moment, Cyril," said Marcella.   "If
all this is true, your young mistress may soon
need friends.   You know where to find me;
I trust you to let me know of her welfare,
and anything else that may be necessary."

When Marcella and the slave parted, the
former turned and threaded the narrow street
that led into that part of the city called the
Sburras, containing the dwellings of the low-
est of the people—mere rows of huts or

hovels, inhabited by the fossi or common laborers, who dug out the tufa, a kind of sand which soon hardened into stone, and was used for most of the buildings in the city. The pits formed by these excavations extended to an immense distance, forming the labyrinth of passages and cells now known as the Catacombs. It was among these men, rude, ignorant, and miserable, that Christianity had made the greatest progress. So infinitely removed from the proud patrician, whose palaces and baths they had built, the Roman noble little cared whether they worshipped Jupiter or Christ, if, indeed, he did not think them too degraded to have any ideas upon the subject. And yet these people did more for the church of Christ than all her powerful enemies could do against her. Their pure and holy lives were living testimonials to the new doctrine. Proof against all temptations, they had concealed in the artificial caves, with which they and they alone were well acquainted, those who were obliged to flee from the rage of their persecutors ; nourishing them for months, until the storm had passed over, and they might return in safety to their homes. The other class in which Christians were mostly found was that composed of slaves and freedmen. Some, indeed, like Marcus the vintner, were independent, and owners of property, but they were few ; and in the higher classes the converts were fewer still. Now, however, there seemed to be a spirit of inquiry arising among the nobler families, and Paulina was not the only one who, in the palaces of Rome, bowed to a crucified Redeemer. For some years they had enjoyed perfect tranquillity, meeting week after week in their little chapels unmolested, so that the younger and more thoughtless part believed the age of persecutions to be past. But keener minds thought differently.

They already saw signs of a coming tempest. They could almost foretell the time when it would burst upon them. They knew that attention had lately been drawn to them by several notable conversions ; one noble had even declared publicly in the senate that the emperor was about to investigate the matter ; and now that Sergius Pollonius had become incensed by the loss of his lawsuit on their account, there was but little doubt that the machinations of so powerful a man would bring them some injury, and that his rancor would certainly increase when he heard that his only child had been seduced to join the company of those he so hated and despised.

The thought of the timid girl exposed to her father's rage made Marcella's heart beat fast for sympathy as she pressed on down the street. Passing through many lanes and alleys, with which she seemed perfectly famil-iar, she stopped at the door of a house which, though of no better materials than the rest, had an air of neatness about it that few of them possessed. Some children who were playing about the door soon recognized her, and ran eagerly toward her, clinging to her gown and hiding their little mud-stained faces in its folds. She had scarcely had time to answer them by a gentle caress, before a man appeared in the doorway, and, with a face expressive of wonder and pleasure, invited her to enter.

"Ah! lady, how good of you!" he said, pushing open the wooden door, and attempting to relieve her of one of the clinging little ones. "The mother is longing much to see you; she has been very low in the night. Let the lady pass, I tell thee, Rufus; is she to step over thee and the threshold too?"

But Marcella had already lifted the child, and with him in her arms entered the room. It was low-ceiled, windowless, and floored by

the bare earth. The only furniture was a
couple of beds, a brazier of lighted charcoal,
a table, and a few stools. By the side of the
fire knelt a young girl of perhaps twelve
years of age, busily engaged in cooking something over the smouldering coals. She was a
quaint, elf-like child, with an old look in her
small face, black, furtive eyes, an immense
quantity of straight black hair, and hands that
went about their work so nimbly and deftly
that it must have been a very active as well
as a practised brain that controlled their
movements.

She glanced up from her work at the darkening of the door, and a deep tinge of red
dyed her usually sallow cheeks, but she did
not speak; she only bent lower over her pot,
and stirred more diligently. Marcella took
no notice of her, but passed directly to the
widow's bedside and spoke to her. She gave
her the alms sent her by the Lady Paulina,

4

but received her grateful expressions with rather an abstracted air, and after a few minutes rose, and, beckoning to the young man to follow her, went out again into the street.

"Mutius," she said, "there is much for us to do—work for all calling themselves Christians. There are stern times at hand; are you ready to act your part?"

He looked up attentively, but not in surprise.

"Yes, lady, I know what you mean; there are to be more witnesses to the faith. I have thought so for some time past. But has the emperor issued an edict!"

"Not yet, but it may come any hour; we must be ready. There must be provision in the retreat; there will be many to need it."

"I will go this very day to the farmers on the Campagna, and have the food ready in the tomb by the temple-pit," said the young man, drawing tighter the leathern belt which confined his tunic, as if to prepare for instant service ; but Marcella laid a hand upon his arm.

"Stay a moment, Mutius ; that is not what I want you most for. We must find out first where the blow is likely to fall, before we can make preparation to endure it or ward it off. I heard it was your witness in the lawsuit of the senator Orinus which lost the case to Sergius Pollonius ?"

"Yes, lady, so they say. It was about the baths they were building side by side, and which were burnt not long ago. I told but the truth, lady—Christ's truth, nothing more."

"Did they not tempt you with gold, Mutius ?"

The young carpenter's face flushed, and his brow knit.

"They did, lady, with gold enough to buy for me what I want most in the world."

"And you would not take it ?"

" I could not sell the truth for gold."

" Not even for little Tullia's sake, Mutius ? "

The young man's head bent lower, and he pulled nervously at the strap of his belt.

" Christ's truth is not bought, lady, neither can it be sold, even for what is brightest and best in our eyes.　Tullia and I can wait his pleasure."

Marcella's eyes glistened as the young man looked up in her face, so humbly, so respectfully, yet as if certain of finding sympathy there.　Nor was he mistaken.　Although the Roman maiden, first schooled in the intricate philosophies of Greek intellect, and then ennobled by Christianity, was little moved by the passions and pleasures which so generally absorb those of her age ; although the circle in which her thoughts and aspirations moved was lifted far above the trivial round of petty cares and trials and joys which formed the world of those around her, yet she was thoroughly a woman, and it was a loving woman's heart shining out of those beautiful eyes that Mutius looked up to with such simple confidence. Although in habits of thought and feeling she stood so entirely alone, although to no mortal ear had she ever revealed herself or displayed the inmost recesses of her spirit, all hearts opened themselves to her. Not only did the timid or doubtful come to her for advice, and the mourners for comfort, but there was scarcely a joy or a hope among those who knew her, which was not confided to her safe and sympathizing guardianship. The mother's rejoicing over her new-born babe, was not complete until it had been shown to Marcella. The bashful, awkward young fossi and freedmen came to narrate to her the difficulties which hindered their course of true love from running smooth; and, with blushing faces, the maidens of their choice sought her ready ear, in which to pour out the story of their new happiness. And for each she had her word of counsel or congratulation. She was never indifferent, she never forgot the least circumstance of the case, but was always ready to enter into each, as if it were the only one before her; and she brought to each such clear perception of character, such delicate tact, and such an unbiassed judgment, that two or three words from her lips seemed to dispel doubts and subdue difficulties which they had been long unsuccessfully combating.

And so it was that she had known long ago the young carpenter's love for the Lady Paulina's little maid, and how nobly the young man had given up the hope of soon bringing home his bride, when his sister's widowhood obliged him to use his earnings for the support of her and her little ones. Thus she could well understand the temptation which had tried him, and she rejoiced that he had passed through it unscathed. But she did not tell him so; words of direct praise seldom fell from her lips, or direct blame still more rarely. It was more by look, tone, and manner, that she conveyed the rebuke or the approbation which was of such importance to all those who came within the sphere of her influence. So she only replied in words of Scripture: "'Commit thy way unto the Lord, and he will bring it to pass.' But, Mutius, did you know that loss of his lawsuit has roused the anger of Sergius Pollonius against all the Christians, and that he is taking measures to induce the emperor to issue an edict against them?"

"Yes, I thought as much, for I was working to-day in the new forum when he and several of the senators passed by, talking very earnestly about it, and they said that the new law would mostly take hold of those who had seduced others from the old relig-

ion ; and they talked of lions in the Colos-
scum, and the boiling baths. Oh ! they all
know you and fear you, lady ! They will
seek you first ! "

The Roman maiden smiled.

" That must not be our first thought,
Mutius ; there are other lives more precious
to the church."

Mutius looked as if he doubted that, but
answered : " You mean the bishop ? but I
have warned him ; he passed through the
forum just after the senators ; it is you we
must save. Oh ! what would we do without
you ! " and the young man stooped and kissed
the hem of her garment.

Marcella drew back instantly, her face
flushing with a stern displeasure the young
carpenter had never seen there before, and
he begged pardon very humbly. " But, O
lady ! you cannot tell how the people in the
Via Aureum love you. Your very shadow

lights up their dark homes like the sun-beams!"

"Hush!" said Marcella; but her face soft-ened a little. "You do not know what you say; but now listen to me. The Lady Pau-lina is about to profess herself a Christian."

The man looked up much astonished.

"The Lady Paulina! They say that Otho-ric, the Gallic chief, asked her in marriage of her father this very day; it was the talk among the nobles in the forum about the splendid gifts he would bestow, and the im-portance of having him for an ally in case of future wars in Germany. They will never let her be a Christian!"

"I did not know of that," replied Marcella, sadly, "but I have long expected something of the kind. Sergius Pollonius has lost so much money by gambling and his lawsuits that he would be glad to find a son-in-law who would give instead of requiring a dower,

4*

and he would do anything to gratify the emperor, and so obtain power. We must all pray for her, Mutius, that her faith fail not in this great trial, and be ready to aid her by actions as well as by prayers. She may soon need a refuge, and a secret one. What I wish you to do is to keep up communication with Cyril, so that through you he may send me word of any danger. The decisive moment may be to-night. That is all now, but I wish to speak to Rhoda—where is she?"

The strange, wild-looking child had, during the whole conversation, been crouched down just inside the door, drinking in every word that had been said : but as soon as she heard her own name mentioned, she stole back again to her pot so swiftly and quietly that, when Mutius went in to find her, he did not imagine that she had ceased her occupation for a moment. She did not seem much inclined for the proposed conversation, as might be seen from the pettish way in which she drew her shoulder from his grasp.

"I cannot come, Mutius. The broth will be spoiled, and what will the mother say then? Let the lady go, I want not her, nor she me."

"But I do want you, poor child," said Marcella's gentle voice, for she had followed Mutius into the room, and having signed to him to go away, laid her hand on the tangled mass of hair which, unconfined by band or comb, hung down, elf-like, over her sunburnt shoulders. The child seemed to shudder at her touch. Marcella felt it, and withdrew her hand instantly, but stood quite still with a look of pain and anxiety on her face. After a few moments, during which the child went on with her operations as if no one was present, she spoke again, but her tone was very humble and sad.

"Will you never let me love you, Rhoda?"

" No."

The word was pronounced with decision, but also with utter indifference.

" Why not, Rhoda ? you poor, unhappy, friendless child. For the Master's sake, whose little lost lamb you are, I must pity you, I must love you."

The beautiful eyes were full of tears, the voice was one of the deepest compassion and tenderness, but neither sight nor sound moved the strong composure of the child. She only glanced up, with an expression of curiosity and distrust in her twinkling, bead-like eyes, then began to break up bits of charcoal, and thrust them under the pot to steady it among the flames.

" Do you remember, Rhoda, the day Mutius brought you here from the Campagna, where you had been left to die ? Do you remember how kindly the widow Susa bathed your poor, bruised, bleeding back, and how the children cried when they said that you could never grow up tall and straight as they might, and how Mutius walked all the way to my home after his hard day's work to get the grapes that you cried for in your fever?"

The child might have been alone in the room for all the consciousness she showed of any one's presence. Marcella paused, wounded and surprised, but in a moment tried another subject.

"Do you know that we may soon need to cling together very closely? There are dark days coming for the Christian church—days of trial and deep affliction, death, and sufferings far worse than death."

For the first time the child looked up, keen, curious, interested; for the first time she spoke.

"Is the emperor going to kill all the Christians?"

"As many as he can, no doubt; we must

pray to our Master to give us strength to endure."

" I hope he will kill them all," said the girl bitterly; " I hate them all! That is good news!" and lifting her pot from the fire, with one of her swift movements she glided past Marcella, carefully avoiding to touch her garments, and escaped through the open door into the winding alleys.

Marcella followed, not attempting to overtake the fugitive, but turning her steps toward home. She looked very sad, and very much perplexed. This was a new and painful experience for her. Love and reverence had come to her so spontaneously from all those with whom she had come in contact, that this child's aversion and malice were both unaccountable and exquisitely painful. She had become deeply interested in the miserable child whom Mutius had found out on the open Campagna, suffering from cruel bruises, cold and hunger, and whom she had assisted to nurse and feed back to life. When the child had recovered after weeks of unconsciousness and delirium, she refused to give any account of herself, or else had forgotten all her previous history; and she became a sore trouble to her kind protectors. Not that she was unwilling to take her part in the household labor; her neatness, readiness and dispatch made her a valuable assistant; but she was so strange, so changeable, so mysterious, and at times so malicious, that she often tried them greatly. When the other children gathered around Marcella's knees to hear her stories from the Bible, Rhoda—for so they had named her, she never would tell her real name—would make such a clattering with the furniture as to drown her voice, or, taking up the broom of twigs, would raise such a cloud of dust from the earthen floor as to drive them away; or, if all

this failed, would shout out some wild, monotonous chant in an unknown tongue, which
made it impossible for any one to hear. To
kindness she was utterly indifferent; of
threats she took no more notice than of
the wind.

But the painful look died away from Marcella's face after a while, and was succeeded
by one of deep thought. Mutius' words,
"They know you, they will seek you first,"
rose up in her mind, but they produced no
fear, rather exultation. She had no fear of
death; a martyr's crown had been too long
the subject of her most earnest aspirations
for her to dread the approach of the martyr's
sufferings; but many things seemed press-
ing upon her, much work seemed left to be
accomplished before she could rest—if they
would only give her time! Not that life
did not beat strongly in her breast; she was
too healthy in mind and body to have morbid

longings for death, and was too unselfish to wish to cast her burdens on others' shoulders. She had strong ties to bind her to earth, but stronger ones that drew her to heaven; and so, willing to stay, glad to depart, she felt that she could lay aside all personal thoughts in the coming struggle, and act only for the welfare of those she loved, and the glory of her Master's kingdom.

So from that day forth she gave but little thought to her impending danger. There were only certain hours, which she spent alone in the quiet of her own room, or the seclusion of the little chapel, that she allowed her mind to dwell on her probable future. None knew what were the inward wrestlings between the brave spirit and the shrinking flesh; only when she came forth there was a holy light about her—a new, unearthly brilliancy in her glorious eyes—that made her friends wonder and be silent.

CHAPTER IV.

Out into the Night.

PAULINA, after her friend's departure, left the saloon in which she had been sitting, and entered an apartment at the side. It was a bedroom furnished with the same lavish expenditure as the rest of the house, It was only lighted by a window looking into the atrium, and that was so shaded by heavy curtains that it would have been almost dark, had it not been illuminated by several bronze and gold lamps hanging from the ceiling, in which the perfumed oil, slowly wasting away, diffused not only light, but a delicious fragrance around the room. Beautifully carved arm-chairs, and tables curiously wrought in wood, metal, and ivory, almost cumbered the chamber, and mirrors of burnished silver, set in the panels of the wall, multiplied many times the scene. Statues in bronze and marble, the work of the greatest artists of the age, looked down from many a niche and pedestal; but perhaps the most beautiful of all the articles of furniture in the room was the bed. It was made of ebony and ivory, inlaid with gold and silver. At the head, an ivory statue of the goddess of Sleep, wreathed with poppies, held one finger to her lips as if enjoining silence, while the other hand grasped the ring from which blue curtains fell in folds to the floor. At the foot, on a shorter pedestal, stood Psyche, bearing in one hand a silver lamp, burning, like the rest, perfumed oil, and with the other pointing upward. The bed-coverings were of blue, embroidered with gold, and bordered by a fringe of the same.

But for all this magnificence the Lady Paulina cared very little; not beçause she had
risen above it, but because from its very
familiarity it had become a matter of indifference to her. She had not, indeed, any idea
of what it was to be without it. All her life
she had not known a wish that could not be
gratified by a touch of her little silver bell.
Her mother had died when she was but an
infant, and her foster-mother had been the
wife of Marcus the vintner. Her father, as
soon as the influence of his wife was removed, had plunged into all kinds of excess, and was only restrained from utter ruin
by his ambition for political power. To
gratify this darling passion he sometimes sacrificed others almost equally beloved. He
could calm his burning hate, smother his
rage, turn from the untasted wine-cup, be
deaf to the solicitations of his licentious companions, if by so doing he could draw him-

self one step nearer, either in fancy or reality, to the grand object of his ambition—the imperial purple. Nor did this idea appear entirely without foundation. In his veins flowed the blood of the Cæsars, only mingled with that of families older and equally distinguished. His wealth, until he squandered it in his schemes, was immense, his eloquence considerable. He did not, it is true, possess the love of the people, but he gained what is to many men as useful, their hearty dread. Until within the last few months Fortune had seemed to favor him, not a single scheme had miscarried, not a single venture but had been crowned with abundant success; but now the fickle goddess seemed determined to prove her right to her ascribed character, and be as much his enemy as she had formerly been his friend. She played him false at the gambling-table, in the senate-chamber, in the emperor's court. He began to hear murmurs of discontent where before had been only silent, cringing submission; and last of all, his lawsuit, involving not only vast sums of money, but also his personal honor, had been decided in favor of a younger aspirant for public favor.

But in all this darkness there was one gleam of light. A Gallic prince, possessing immense tracts of territory, and exercising great influence over the affairs of those northern nations which were even then becoming formidable to Rome, had been fascinated by the sweet face of the Lady Paulina, and offered to unite with him in his schemes against the Christians, whom he imagined to be the cause of his dangerous position, if he would give him his daughter in marriage. He was inspirited by this proffered assistance, for he might in this way, not only gratify his ambition, but also his malice, his revenge, and his cruelty. He laid his plans with the greatest caution. All the powers of his naturally fine mind were invoked to plot and counterplot; and now he had just left the emperor's private audience-chamber, after witnessing the signing of an edict which, if properly enforced, as he meant it should be, would wipe out the name of Christian from the annals of Rome.

Such was the parent to whom this timid, shrinking girl must confess that she had cast in her lot with the despised and hated sect. No wonder she sank down by the side of her bed, and buried her face in its drapery.

"Strength, O Lord! strength!" was the cry of that weak, trembling spirit, sinking at the very thought of the magnitude of the trial which awaited her. Well for her that she knew where to appeal for protection in this her hour; well for her that supernatural strength was at hand. Prayer calmed her, soothed her, so gently that she could hardly tell how it was accomplished ; the Comforter came to her, and in the arms of his love she sank like a wearied, frightened child. Gradually her sobs grew fainter and ceased, her quivering nerves relaxed, and her face, sweet and sad, but peaceful, resting on her clasped hands—she slept.

The twilight was deepening in the shaded chamber when she awoke, recalled to the present by her maid Tullia, who informed her that her father commanded her presence that evening at the arena or supper, which was even then being served. She arose bewildered and dizzy; she could only remember that something very dreadful was about to happen, without being able to comprehend what it was. Slowly it all dawned upon her, and opening wide her frightened eyes, she made an involuntary movement as if about to run from the threatened danger, before she realized the uselessness of such an attempt. Then, with instinctive wisdom, she gave herself no further time for thought, but only staying to dip her hand in an alabaster vase of perfumed water, which a Parian nymph held out for her refreshment, and press it for a moment over her brow and eyes, she passed out into the atrium.

It was the hour for the principal meal of the day, on which the Roman, cook bestowed all his skill. It was not often that Paulina was called upon to partake of this with her father, as he was generally accompanied by his political friends, who were neither fit nor agreeable companions for a modest maiden; and she well knew that this summons betokened he was alone, and had some important communication to make. At any other time her girlish curiosity would have been aroused, but now her mind was so pre-occupied by the disclosure she had to make that she scarcely gave the subject a thought, but followed the slave sent to conduct her to the dining-hall.

For some time the meal progressed in silence, the father seemed in no mood for conversation, the daughter, although the important declaration rose many times to her lips, could not compose her trembling voice to utter it. The well-trained slaves glided noiselessly about their respective tasks, the rare and costly viands in gold and silver dishes were brought in and removed, most of them untasted, with the wines proper for each, and of these alone the master of the house had partaken freely. His movements became very abrupt and restless; more than once the stately Nubian, who stood at the back of the couch on which he reclined, was obliged to pick up and replace the cushion which supported his left elbow. At length, when the fruit alone remained on the table, and all the servants had, at their master's

signal, left the room, the Roman noble spoke:
"Paulina, the great Gallic chief, Orthorix,
is high in favor with the emperor."

There was no answer, only a look of surprise in the brown eyes; so he took another
draught of the fiery Falernian wine, and then
continued:

"He will sup with me to-morrow night,
and it is my will that you be present and
receive him. Wear the jewels that I bought
of the Jew Solomon in Eygpt."

The maiden still gazed in her father's face
in mute interrogation, all this seemed so
strangely irrelevant to the thoughts then
occupying her mind. Pollonius' brow grew
dark at the sight of her innocent face, still
darker at the reply which came at length:

"Is he a good man, father?"

The noble took another draught from his
golden cup, vexed at the question put in such
a point-blank manner. *Good* he knew very

well he was not, but moral character was an aspect under which he had not thought of viewing his future son-in-law.

"Good or not, what matters it?" he said at length. "He has asked you of me in marriage."

The color rushed painfully into the young girl's face and neck, and her hand trembled as she caught hold of the arm of the couch to steady herself. She saw that her father had decided her future for her; she did not think of such a thing as turning him from his purpose. It was not the custom for maidens to have any voice in this most momentous decision; they were seldom allowed to become acquainted with those who were to be their companions through life, until the deed was consummated and their husbands lifted them over the thresholds into their future homes. So Paulina was not as much astonished at this abrupt declaration as a maiden of modern times would be; the great question with her was how this change would affect her Christian life; and hardly knowing what she did, she put the thought that was uppermost in her mind into words.

"My father, is he a Christian?"

The astonished Roman put down the goblet he had just raised to his lips, his face reddening with surprise and wrath—wrath at the associations connected with the hated name, surprise at the strangeness of the question.

"By Jove and all the gods!" he exclaimed, starting up from his couch, "were he ten, ay, a hundred times as rich as he is, if he were a Christian dog he should have no daughter of mine. No, he serves the gods of his ancestors, and knows nothing of all this foolery. But where did you learn anything of this upstart deceiver?" And here followed a string of oaths and imprecations fearful for any one to hear, terrible indeed for the shuddering, trembling child before him; but in the midst she sprung to her feet. The most timid animal will dare resist when those it loves most are assailed, and the sound of those horrid words applied to him who was so very dear to her made her forget all fear.

"Father! father! you must not speak so. He is so good and kind and holy! He is my God! I love him; I am a Christian!"

It was strange to see the change that came over the bloated, sensual face of the haughty Roman. Passions so various, so violent, so conflicting, swept over it in such rapid succession that its convulsive movements more resembled those of a demon, thwarted and brought to bay, than of a human being. But it was over in a moment, only leaving a look of bitter defiance and hatred on his pale lips and darkened brow; but he trembled from head to foot, trembled as his daughter did not, though she stood before him with all the weight of his fierce wrath upon her. For Marcella had prophesied truly; in the moment of her trial came the needed strength. Weakness and fearfulness disappeared before the magic of that loved name. The magnificent apartment, with its paintings and sculpture and perfumed air, even her angry father, faded away from her sight, and she only saw one loving, sympathizing face looking down upon her, she only heard one gentle voice making music in her ears, she only felt one strong, encircling arm on which she rested, and was safe. She heard, as if they came from very far away, the curses that her father poured out upon her; she hardly felt his rough grasp when at last, moved beyond all endurance by the passive silence of the girl before him, he dragged her to her own apartment and thrust her in.

Then, after awhile, she came slowly back to the present; her supernatural strength was

gone, and she was once more the timid, shrinking girl, shuddering at the .past and cowering
before the future. She remembered now her
father's terrible sentence, from which she felt
no human power could induce him to retract ;
one week of solitary confinement, in which to
decide whether she would abjure Christ and
sacrifice to the gods, or be turned from the
door, a homeless outcast, to brave as she
might the fury of the emperor's new edict.

It was pitiful to see her as she stood there,
her hair thrown back from her forehead, her
pale lips quivering, her hands clasping each
other convulsively, her eyes, dilated and tear-
less, with their peculiar, hunted expression,
wandering from side to side, as if in search of
some friend, some comfort, some hope in this
dark, dark hour. But there was none to see,
none to hear the low moan of anguish with
which she threw herself down on her bed ;
no one to press a gentle, cooling hand upon

those throbbing temples; no one to whom she could cling and tell all those nervous terrors which her state of excitement made particularly hard to bear, but which would have vanished before a word of kindly sympathy. Human aid there was none, but the Good Shepherd had not forgotten his feeble lamb. "As one whom his mother comforteth," so comforted he the desolate child; and when Pollonius, after drowning whatever remorse he may have felt in the wine-cup, was led, cursing and shouting, to his room by his slaves, she was sleeping with such a happy smile on her face as even her most joyous moments seldom brought there.

How she passed those weary seven days that succeeded this night, she never could exactly tell. Sometimes she played with her birds, or watched the gold fish in the fountain, clapping her hands with childish glee as she watched their sports, forgetting for a few mo-

5*

ments her own troubles; but then, again, they would come upon her in their full weight, and sometimes a faint hope would cross her mind that her father would not execute his fearful threat, that he only meant to frighten and punish her, and then he would forgive her; and perhaps, if he gave her to Orthorix, the Gaul might be kind to her far away in her northern home. Then the thought would come that all her friends had forsaken her, and she would go and sit down by the barred door, and listen for hours to the occasional footsteps in the atrium, hoping each one might be Marcella's. She did not know that the fearless maiden had twice braved her father's wrath in her behalf; that Cyril and her little maid Tullia watched night and day by turns the door which they were forbidden to enter, and never ceased their prayers for her to the only one who could aid. She took little note of time; it seemed months to her before the eighth day arrived, and the grave steward came to lead her to her father's presence. He found her sunk in a state of deep apathy, but she started and shivered at the sound of his voice breaking on her long silence, and followed him without a word, walking feebly, and tottering so that more than once she grasped at the marble columns in the atrium to save herself from falling.

Sergius Pollonius looked up as his daughter entered, and was for one moment shocked at the effect of his cruel punishment; but in another wrath overpowered remorse, for he saw that his plan had failed. He saw in those dimmed, sunken eyes, patient endurance, but no submission ; in the pale cheeks suffering, but no yielding. Disappointed and baffled, hatred and cruelty smothered in his breast any faint feelings that might have been left there of parental love and tenderness. Still he spoke calmly.

"Paulina, you have had time to think, to decide. What have you to say?"

"Father, I cannot deny Him. Forgive me, have mercy! I will obey you in everything else, but how can I deny my Saviour?"

"Hark you, girl," cried the Roman, his tone rising as his smothered wrath burst forth, "my word is passed; it shall be as I said; one word, and you leave my roof forever. Choose now between your God and your home, ay, and your life. Choose now and forever!" he thundered when she did not answer at once.

She crossed her hands meekly upon her throbbing bosom, and uttered one word, "Christ."

There was a heavy hand on her shoulder, the door was flung back, and out among the crowd of frightened, staring slaves in the entrance porch, the father drew his child. "Open the gate!" he thundered. The great bronze doors were open in a moment, and the night, in all the blackness of a gathering storm, was before them. Already a few rain-drops dashed in their faces.

The girl saw the terror before her and shrank. She turned and clung to that cruel, pitiless arm.

"O father! not out in the storm, not alone in the night!"

The lines in the hard, brutal face did not soften for an instant. The great bronze doors clanged again, and with one cry of terror the trembling girl fled, homeless, friendless, from her father's door, out into the darkness and the storm of a cruel world.

CHAPTER V.

The Storm Gathering.

THE week following the signing of the new edict was a very quiet one, as until the expiration of that time it was not to be enforced. It was directed chiefly against those who had attempted to convert others to their religion, but was so loosely expressed that it might be brought to bear upon any poor Christian who might chance to incur the displeasure of some one more powerful than himself. The accuser might also, by convicting him of the crime, obtain half his property. This was particularly pleasing to many of the profligate young nobles who had wasted their patrimony in the riotous pleasures of the

court, and who were now so pressed by creditors as scarcely to know which way to turn.
Many a longing gaze was cast by these needy
young patricians, as they reeled home from
their orgies, at the peaceful faces of the
Christians, then just repairing to their daily
toil, as serene and unconscious as though the
thunders of the Roman law were not about to
burst on their unprotected heads. There
were many stories floating about of immense
treasure hid by the despised sect in the catacombs, and their enemies could hardly re-
strain their impatience for the trials to begin
that they might take possession.

Of all this the Christians were aware, and
quietly and secretly they made what preparations they could to endure, not resist, the
storm. Some few left the city, but they were
very few. The bishop, and some of the older
ones among the clergy, took up their resi-
dence in the retreats among the catacombs;

but most of them went on very quietly with their daily work.

In the household of Marcus the vintner there seemed to be little or no change, none that their young guests could perceive. Marcus himself labored as diligently among the vines as though he expected to gather in the fruits, and his wife went about the house, keeping it in even more than its usual dainty order, with cheerful voice and practiced hand. It may have been that the father, returning home from his work in the evening, clasped his boys to his breast with unusual emotion; it may have been that the mother, hushing the baby on her knee with a Christian hymn for a lullaby, dropped a tear on its unconscious face, and thought of Rachael and her children; but their high and simple faith forbade any lamentation or despair; having the Lord on their side they did not fear what man might do unto them.

As for Marcella, she went on her daily round of love and charity exactly as usual. She must have seen the looks which were cast upon her as she passed along the streets, lingering looks of tenderness from the old and feeble, of earnest, sadly affectionate reverence from the strong and sturdy workers ; but she heeded them not. Wherever there was a deed of mercy to be performed, there she was to be found, calm, cool, collected, knowing just what to do, never shrinking from doing it. Only in one thing she varied from her usual routine, she took less rest. The first gray streaks of the dawn found her among the mud-cottages of the sburri, far more welcome there than even the sunbeams ; and it was only the solemn stars which lighted her home through the deserted streets as she returned from the bedside of the sick and the dying. Her parents understood her too well to expostulate. Duty shone out in all its fair proportions, illuminated by the light of the rapidly approaching eternity. Father, mother, and daughter realized perfectly that they were, in all probability, passing their last days together on earth; but this knowledge only showed itself in a more particular attention to the little courtesies of daily life, mute caresses from hearts too full for utterance, a whispered text, and a trembling blessing.

Of all this their guests saw little or nothing. The religion they despised had never been forced upon their attention. Eudora, always gay and communicative, had formed a friendship with almost all the maidens in the neighborhood, and had now gone to visit other friends. Philip remained, pleased with the quiet he found there, which his sister could hardly endure. He was very much aroused by the wonders which surrounded him in the world-famed city, and a variety of new ideas had invaded his indolent mind. But beyond all palaces, tombs, and triumphal arches, he admired his cousin Marcella. Not only her beauty pleased his critical taste, but her high and holy life seemed to him to fulfil the dreams of his native poets and philosophers. He liked to fancy her some one of the divinities in human shape, yet she seemed to go beyond them all. He could not discover the secret springs of her life. Open and transparent as were all her actions, the motives which induced them were a mystery to him. Nor was all this made easier to understand by a discovery he made that week. One so much absorbed in reveling in the feast spread out before his intellect and fancy would not be very likely to notice the putting forth of the edict against an obscure sect, the very name of which he sought to banish from his mind. He was standing in the portico of a temple which was being repaired, contemplating a statue to which the artist was putting a few finishing touches, when Marcella passed by. He was hidden by a pillar, so that she did not see him, but he noticed how one of the roughest of the workmen sprang forward to remove a tool which lay in her way, and how they all ceased work until she had passed out of sight, with such reverence in their looks and attitudes as he had never seen shown to the greatest of the nobles. Moved by curiosity, he approached the laborers and inquired:

"Do you know the name of the maiden who just passed?"

The men looked at him in wonder for a moment, then the one who had removed the the tool from her path said:

"You must be a stranger in Rome, young sir, if you know not Marcella; every one knows her!"

"Not the great nobles," said another workman, his grim, toil-stained face lighting up with a look of triumph; "not the nobles, they have nothing to do with her ; the emperor is not rich enough to buy her from us ; she belongs to us, the people!"

"She belongs to every one that is in trouble," said the first speaker. "She is like the sunshine to us, she warms and cheers us all. The rich shut it out of their houses that they .may burn perfumed oil in golden lamps, but it is all we have in our dark homes!"

Philip hardly liked this appropriation of his cousin, but he wished to try them a little further.

"She is very beautiful."

The workman stood leaning on his pick, one brawny hand shading his eyes that he might peer down the street where Marcella had stopped to pick up and comfort a little crying child. He turned round to the young Greek with a look as though the thought had never crossed his mind before, and then said simply: "They say she is, but I never thought about it. Wormwood is bitter from a golden cup, and honey sweet from a clay one; she is Marcella. What matters it?"

Philip was turning away, disgusted with people so little capable of appreciating beauty, when a detaining hand was laid on his shoulder.

"Who art thou that askest thus after our maiden? If thou art one of those come to spy out her ways and bring her before the judges, it were better for thee to keep out of the way of the fossi!"

The place was lonely, the men had gathered around him with threatening looks; at another time he would have imagined that it lowered his dignity to confess himself related to one whom the common people seemed to appropriate so entirely to themselves; but he was not very brave, and with his cheeks a shade paler than usual he placed his back against a pillar and waved them back with an imperious motion of his hand.

"Back, fellows! I am no spy on her actions or yours; I am her kinsman."

The men fell back, but still doubtful, and muttering.

"Kinsman in blood, but not in soul or faith," said the chief speaker, taking up his pick again: and Philip made his way as fast as possible toward a part of the city where he would find more agreeable society.

His courage rose again when he found himself in the Via Sacra. He felt sure that Marcella was entirely unaware of the danger to which she was exposed, and he thought it would be a very pleasant thing to have those beautiful eyes turned appealingly to him for protection; he entirely forgot how impossible it would be to afford her that protection. When it did occur to him that his single arm would be rather feeble against the weight of the emperor's edict, backed by the invincible hosts of Rome, his fancy only took a different track, and showed him the beautiful maiden, convinced of the follies into which her enthusiasm had led her, renouncing her absurd creed, offering a sacrifice to the gods of her ancestors, and then leaving the city where each dirty fossus claimed her as friend and sister, to go back with him to his Grecian home, to revel undisturbed in tranquil dreams of love and philosophy. Full of these thoughts he awaited impatiently her return in the evening and met her in the garden-path.

"Marcella!" he cried, in a tone of such trembling earnestness that she looked at him with surprise and anxiety, wondering what this could mean from one who seemed in his life to unite the luxuriousness of the Epicureans with the indifference of the Stoics. "Marcella! you do not know you are in great danger; they wish to bring you before the judges; the emperor has sent out an edict against the Christians, and they will seek you first."

He expected to see her at least turn pale at this sudden announcement, but she only smiled.

"This is no news to me, Philip; I have known it a long while."

He stood perfectly aghast. Known it a long while! Could it be possible that she had passed in and out before him all these days so perfectly calm, nay cheerful, with the knowledge of this terrible danger hanging over her?

"But you do not know, you surely cannot understand; have you thought that this is death?"

"No, Philip; but I have thought that it is immortality."

"Marcella! for pity's sake do not keep up this delusion any longer. Whatever these

6

fancies may do for you in daily life, they will not avail you now. The dead Nazarene can do nothing against the Emperor of Rome. All your doctrines together cannot blunt the points of swords or shut the mouths of hungry lions. What can your hope do in the face of all this?"

She was silent for a moment. Philip thought he had convinced her. When she did speak, her tone was very gentle.

"Philip! you ask what my hope is now? I tell you it is firmer than ever before, for the waves of this fierce storm are breaking upon it, and it does not even tremble. Christ is not the dead Nazarene, he is the risen God; the emperor himself is not his unwilling servant. I do not mean that I expect a miracle, although by one word he could dismay all the Roman hosts. I fully expect to die, and I do not fear death."

"But death is such a fearful thing," said

the young man, shuddering. "Decay and worms to the body, annihilation, perhaps, to the soul, oblivion certainly for both. Our greatest philosophers could only say that the future of the soul is so doubtful that it were better to cease to be than to look forward to such vague uncertainty—mystery shrouded in mystery. O Marcella, you are too young to die!"

Philip's face was flushed with unusual emotion, for this was a subject on which he had thought long and deeply. His poetical, imaginative nature had yearned for immortality; for something toward which to look when the few short years allotted to man on the earth were accomplished; something besides forgetfulness, decay, nothingness; but he had never found it. There were the old fables of Tartarus and the Elysian fields, and a few hopes, expressed by Plato and Socrates, that the soul, being an emanation from Deity, would either be reabsorbed by Deity, or else continue to enjoy an existence very different from life, but still not painful. And this was all the comfort that paganism had to offer to one standing in the presence of a fearful death. Well was it for the Roman maiden that she had a better hope. And oh! how brightly faith and joy and tender compassion beamed in those dark eyes, as she gave a reason for that hope within her!

Philip listened astonished, awe-struck, entranced. A heaven so tangible that its very gates and walls, its streets and gardens, its inhabitants and their occupations, had been described by one who had actually trodden its glorious precincts, and returned to tell the tale, was indeed a revelation so vast as to strike him dumb with astonishment; but Marcella proceeded, and told him of one who had left all these delights, and come down to earth to suffer and die a shameful death, that its gates might be opened to him, to her, to all; who in himself had tasted death for every man; who, resting for three days in the garden tomb, made all other tombs in the earth only resting-places for weary bodies, where they might sleep sweetly until he came to lead them in triumph to his own beautiful home, where ages on ages would find the soul no nearer the termination of its joys than when it first awaked to a consciousness of them.

We who have been from our cradles accustomed to the full light of this bessed hope of immortality can hardly imagine the sensations of one upon whom it burst for the first time in manhood. For a moment his mind did not ask for proof; thoughts, too many for utterance, were passing through it; his soul was reveling in a hope so new, so entrancing, that it did not care to tear itself away from it in order to examine the foundation on which it was resting. How long it would have been before he awoke from his reverie, and became the cool, reasoning philosopher once more, cannot be told, for at that moment they were interrupted. There was a hasty step up the garden-path, and a slight, girlish figure threw herself, sobbing, into Marcella's arms.

"O Marcella! take me, keep me! I have no home, no father. I am all alone in the night!"

She was trembling from head to foot with cold and terror, and Marcella drew her to a seat, and hushed and soothed as she would have done a frightened child. Philip looked on in amazement; nor was he less surprised when, by the light of the lamps within, he saw her rich yet disordered garments, and the exquisite beauty of the face, heightened by the tear-drops still glistening in her eyes and the bright color imparted to her cheeks by excitement. For some time she could only tremble and sob, and cling to her supporter as if she feared she might be torn away from her at any moment. The hunted, terrified look in her eyes was so apparent that Philip, in compassion, rose and fastened the door, and Marcus came forward and took both her cold hands in his. "Fear not, lady; for this night, at least, thy father will not seek thee, and we shall all receive strength to-morrow."

"My father will never seek me," replied Paulina with a fresh burst of tears. "He sent me away forever out of his doors, into the night and the storm; he had no pity. But, O Marcella! I did not deny Christ! And he helped me all these days to bear it, and not to fear so much at the last."

Philip did not comprehend this, but Marcus did, and his voice trembled with compassion as he placed his hand on the girl's bowed head. "Christ, for whom thou hast left home and friends, will be father, mother, and kinsman in one. Hard indeed is the conflict, but

Christ giveth the victory, and there remain-
eth the rest!"

"But will it be long coming?" said Paulina, looking up in his face with a sad smile
on her pale lips. "I am so weak, I have so
little faith, and I dread it all so. They will
not bring me before the judges? Will they
kill me as they did those we heard of long
ago?"

Marcella clasped her tighter in her arms,
and bending her face over the chestnut curls,
dropped silent tears upon them. She who,
in her lofty, holy courage, looked forward
unflinchingly upon her own approaching suffering, she who had no tears to shed at the
prospect of a death of which strong men
spoke in whispers of horror, wept freely over
this poor, homeless, worse than orphaned
child, who in her weakness and helplessness
must face the stern judges, with whom inno-
cence and beauty would plead in vain.

None of them regained their calmness until after the evening worship, at which Philip was present for the first time. He entirely forgot to leave the room as was his ordinary custom. Then each retired to rest.

Philip threw himself upon his couch, but not to sleep. One grand conviction had stamped itself upon his mind: there must be something in a faith which could thus animate even feeble women and children to yield friends, fortune, and even life itself to maintain it. This was no vague system of morality and philosophy. No philosopher had yet been found so sure of arguments as to be willing to die for them. And the future, immortality, the resurrection of the body, was this a delusion, or was it not that for which the sages of his land had been so long, so vainly seeking? It seemed to him a humiliating thought that what those master-minds had failed to discover had been brought to

6*

light by these unknown Galileans. But then, as if in answer to this thought, came the assertion of Marcella, that God himself had declared all this, having assumed a human form for the very purpose. Man had long tried to discover the secret and had failed. God, who alone knew, had revealed it ; how simply, and yet how perfectly, the want was met by the supply !

Thus battled pagan superstition with the grand Christian doctrine of immortality, and the morning found the conflict still undecided.

In an adjoining chamber Paulina, nestled close in Marcella's protecting arms, told all her story. "It was not I, only Christ," were her last words as she fell asleep.

And Marcella, too, slept calmly and sweetly, the whole great city slept ; and the night passed solemnly on, and the morning dawned.

CHAPTER VI.

Life among the Dead.

MORNING dawned brightly over the great capital of the world. The gates were crowded with peasants entering with their loads of vegetables and fruits, and workmen passing out toward their various places of occupation in the suburbs. There was a burst of martial music from one of the streets leading to the Campus Martius, whither a troop of horse-soldiers were being led for exercise. The shopkeepers were opening their shops, and displaying their wares ready for customers. The bread-sellers had already transacted a good deal of business. Slaves taken from various lands hurried hither and thither on their errands, and in and out of the doors of the countless temples passed throngs of worshippers: the masters of the world had arisen and were astir.

To the casual observer this appeared very much like other days; business and pleasure divided the minds of men as usual, but one looking more closely might have noticed that in many a workshop, and among the piles of stone and mortar incumbering the way where new buildings were in progress, the workmen were absent. This was not on account of the emperor's edict. Each Christian knew that the best way of escaping the danger was to go quietly about his daily work, in the hope that his insignificance would screen him from the hate of his enemies; but whatever might be the consequence of thus openly severing himself from his heathen companions, he could not work on this day, for it was the Christian Sabbath.

Philip did not sleep till daybreak, but when at last nature exerted her authority over the exhausted body and mind, he slept long and heavily. His first thought on waking was to seek Marcella, but she was nowhere to be found. By the position of the sun, he knew that the morning must be far advanced, but the house seemed deserted. Marcus' tools were carefully put away, all the household arrangements were in unusually perfect order. There was no fire burning, even the ashes had been carefully swept away. The doors were wide open, and the cheerful sunlight, flickering through the vines about the porch, seemed trying to make as bright as possible the homely furniture and simple rooms. Bright as was the scene, it struck unpleasantly on Philip's feelings. It did not look as if it were awaiting the joyful return of its occupants, but rather as if those occupants had put it in order for another owner, and left it forever.

He had very little doubt as to where his friends were to be found, and he resolved to seek them instantly. It did not even cross his mind that they had purposely left him, and given him no clue to their present asylum, as being the best means of protecting him from the danger into which his connection with them might bring him. He remembered that it was their day of worship, and he had heard that they sometimes met in the catacombs, so he determined to seek them there, entirely ignorant of the vast extent of this labyrinth, and the difficulty and danger of traversing those gloomy endless passages without a guide. He did not know either the immense number of entrances open and concealed, leading into them; he had heard of one in the vaults of a tomb in the Campagna, and thither he directed his steps.

The tomb was a ruined one, part of the foundation having sunk on account of the excavations beneath it, and it was now used as a depository for the tufa as it was brought to the surface. When he arrived there he was wearied, and sat down on a block of stone to rest, and consider what had best be done next. Something in the shape of his seat made him rise to see what it was that was affording him a resting place. It was a fallen statue of Minos. There lay the grim god, mutilated and half covered with earth, but preserving in his features the expression which denoted his character—justice; but a justice which, though it might be bent by the dictates of passion and revenge, never leaned to the side of mercy. He turned to the walls. The paintings with which they had been adorned were still fresh and distinct. There was Mars drawn in his chariot by Fright and Terror, Discord before him, and Clamor and Anger behind, the bloody-jawed wolf ran at his side, and the raven, perched on his shoulder, stretched forth its ugly head, eager for blood.

Opposite was a festival of Bacchus. The god, nodding with intoxication in the midst of his hideous demons and satyrs, leered at the Bacchantes who, with dishevelled hair and faces stained with the dregs of wine, sang to him their hymns of praise. Philip turned away his eyes, but only to encounter representations of the jealousies of Juno, the vanities of Venus, the thieving of Mercury, the cruelty of Diana, and the various unnatural crimes of the lesser divinities.

"Behold thy gods!" he said to himself. "Such are the Immortals. The best future that the poets and sages of the world could give to their heroes, was to join such companions."

Nor did the thought that the wisest men regarded these things as poetical fables, having deep and subtile meanings, comfort him.

All was vague, uncertain, indefinite. Here he sat, a living, breathing, thinking man; yonder reposed the ashes of one who had once been also a man, but was now so no more. What made the difference between him and yonder handful of dust? What had become of the principle which once made the clay a man?

This grand mystery, too deep for the master-minds of the world to solve, these simple Christians declared they had fathomed. Was this the truth? If it was a delusion, it was the grandest and happiest of delusions. Would that he might be so deluded!

He rose, and after lighting a torch at a neighboring cottage, he descended the roughly cut steps and entered the labyrinth. All was darkness save for the light from the flickering torch which gleamed ruddily on the low-arched ceiling and the contracted walls of the seemingly interminable passage along which he was advancing. He now left the more recently worked galleries, and came to those which, having been long worked out, had been used by Christian and pagan alike as a place of sepulchre. Cavities had been excavated, one above another, on each side, just large enough to contain a single body, and the front had been closed again with a slab of stone, on which some inscription was generally placed. Beside many was a little niche which held a lamp, in some cases kept burning by the care of loving friends, but often extinguished; perhaps overturned, broken and forgotten.

Philip was very much interested, and went on and on, now brushing the dust from some half-erased letters, or raising his torch that he might decipher some oddly expressed inscription overhead.

"I, Procope, lift up my hands against the gods who snatched me away innocent," read one.

"Caius, a servant of Christ, sleeps; he will arise," read another.

"Baths, wine, and lust ruin the constitution, but they constitute life. Farewell, and applaud me."

"Julia, in the peace of the Lord. Victoria rests in the peace of Christ."

Two mothers had laid, side by side, in this dreary abode, the little ones they loved. The old religion had no comfort in this case. Fate—hard, cruel—relentless, had ordained the unnecessary deed; so the broken-hearted mother wrote this over her tomb: "Caius Julius Maximus, Æ. two years and five months. O relentless fortune! why is Maximus so early snatched away from me, he who so lately used to lie in my bosom? This stone now marks his tomb. Behold his mother!"

In ruder characters wrote the tearful, yet rejoicing Christian parent:

" Lawrence, to his sweetest son Severus borne away by angels the ides of January." Beneath was carved a shepherd bearing in his arms a little lamb.

Here truly was the divine love for which Plato had longed—love so powerful as to conquer the fear of death, love so tender as to clasp in its embrace a little dying child.

And on other tombs around were placed marks which Philip could not but understand—rude drawings of the instruments of torture under which the now peaceful sleepers had suffered. Who had ever died for the thief Mercurius, the jealous Jupiter, the cruel Diana, the licentious Bacchus? They had been served from fear, never from love.

But these pictures served also to arouse him from his dreams, and bring him back to the present. Could it be that Marcella was in danger of suffering these fearful torments? Could he save her? Where was she? He raised his torch and looked around him. Blackness and darkness and tombs, above, below, and on either hand ; long, echoing passages opened in all directions ; a deep oppressive stillness was brooding over the heavy air, and his torch was failing.   No wonder that his heart sank and his pulses beat wildly, while the small remnant of burning wood fell from his nerveless grasp, as he saw before him, as though it had sprung from one of the graves, the figure of a child.

It was, indeed, a strange sight that was revealed to him by the light of an antique bronze lamp, evidently taken from one of the tombs.   A child in size and figure, but old in features and expression ; small, bead-like eyes, twinkling from under a mass of tangled hair, her olive skin pale with excitement, her deformed body and disproportioned limbs rendered more repulsive by the suppressed passion which worked in every muscle of face and figure. Philip recoiled a little, and the girl gave a mocking laugh; there was nothing childlike about it.

"You are lost!" said the creature, in a voice as uncouth as her form. "It were a pity if one were missing; follow me."

She turned and sped so rapidly down a dark passage to the right, that Philip, who thought his only chance of ever seeing daylight again was to follow her, could hardly keep her in sight. At length she paused with her light at the top of a stair, and beckoned him on. There was a muffled sound of voices heard when he stood at her side, and eagerly followed with his eyes the direction of her pointing finger; but when he turned to ask her where he was, she had disappeared.

He did not trouble himself about this, however; his thoughts were all engaged on the novel scene before him. As he advanced a few steps the passage widened suddenly into a chamber of nearly circular shape, some thirty feet in diameter. The walls, floor, and arched ceiling were of stone. Opposite him, in a recess, stood a stone table, with stone chairs on either side and a font in front. The light of half a dozen metal lamps, suspended from the ceiling, fell on more than thirty people, men, women, and children, who, having their backs to him, had not noticed his approach. They were seated on benches around the walls, an open space being left in the centre; and the attention of all turned toward the group gathered around the font.

At its foot knelt Paulina, her pure white robes scarcely fairer than her face, from which all color had departed. Her eyes, swollen with weeping, were fastened upon Marcella, who stood at her side with one of her hands clasped in hers, the other was laid in that of the venerable bishop, and she was repeating his words after him in low, trembling tones. It was a vow of renunciation, simple, but very comprehensive; strict enough for the stoic, but undertaken in no stoical spirit. Philip heard and wondered. Where was the strength to come from which would be necessary to keep these solemn promises? There was none in that timid, shrinking, promiser. It was as though an infant were to raise its hand to beat down the iron-clad cohorts of the empire, and expect to gain a victory.

He heard further, and his question was answered. The bishop dipped his hand into the font, and sprinkling the drops on the bowed head, signed on her forehead the sign of the cross. The young Greek shuddered. That sign of ignominy and suffering, on a being so pure, so innocent, and so weak! The bishop's next words came to his ear strange and mysterious; their meaning was more than he could fathom.

" I baptize thee in the name of the Father, the Son, and the Holy Ghost. Be strong in Christ's strength, perfect in his perfectness, glorified in his·glory, that thou mayest so pass through this trouble-filled world, that in the world to come thou mayest have life everlasting!"

As he ended, the old man's hands were pressed on the convert's head, and, with his eyes raised heavenward, he continued a few moments in silent prayer. Then raising the newly baptized, he stooped and kissed her. Marcella, too, embraced her, and led her away to one of the seats, while the bishop, with his attendant ministers, turned toward the altar. A deacon then stepped forward with a roll in his hand, and began to read. He first read St. John's description of the last hours of Christ. The young man's face glowed with feeling as he uttered that master-piece of eloquent tenderness: " Let not your heart be

7

troubled : ye believe in God, believe also in me. In my Father's house are many mansions. I go to prepare a place for you. And if I go and prepare a place for you, I will come again, and receive you unto myself; that where I am, there ye may be also."

Homeless, hunted fugitives, looking forward to a speedy and violent death, these words fell upon their ears with a power which we, in these happier days, can only imagine.

The reader passed on and read passage after passage from the epistles, all bearing on the one grand subject that absorbed every heart—the eternal life. When he had finished, the bishop, rising from his chair, said:

" Lift up your hearts !"

And the answer came from every lip :

" We lift them up unto the Lord."

" Let us give praise unto the Lord."

"It is meet and right so to do," and then all joined the joyful chant:

"Therefore with angels and archangels and with all the company of heaven we laud and magnify thy holy name, ever more praising thee and saying, Holy, holy, holy, Lord God of hosts, the earth is full of thy glory. Glory be to thee, O God most high!"

As the noble strains died away along the vaulted passages the bishop offered the prayer for the church militant. His voice faltered a little as he came to the words: "We also render thanks, O Lord, for all those departed this life in thy faith and fear," as he thought how very soon they might all be called to "follow their good examples, and with them be made partakers of the heavenly kingdom;" but as he passed on to the prayer of consecration, the commemoration of Christ's words, and the oblation, it became firm again.

Philip, meanwhile, was drinking in every

word. Many, very many and strange thoughts were passing through his mind, but they were not sad thoughts. He felt that the depths of his nature were being stirred by a power stronger than his will, that his soul was struggling as for a new birth. Indolence and languor had no longer a place left for indulgence, when an immortal spirit first realized its immortality, and leaped upward to grasp the priceless treasure.

The bread was broken, the Lord's prayer repeated, and the consecrated elements distributed; and so absorbed was he that he did not hear a dull, tramping sound, now advancing, now receding, now again advancing; did not notice that at each of the four arched entrances the light from the lamps gleamed on the burnished armor of a soldier of the royal guard.

CHAPTER VII.

Freedom in Chains.

ON this eventful morning a deep gloom
hung over the palace of Sergius Pollonius in the Via Sacra. Not only in the deserted boudoir where the Cupids and Graces
on the walls smiled uselessly at each other,
not only in the lonely chamber where the
Psyche, with her extinguished lamp, gazed
down as if in wonder on the unused bed, even
in the atrium, bright as it was with sunlight,
the very drops from the fountain plashed
mournfully on the shoulders of the water-
nymphs, and the vines upon the pillars
drooped. And gloomiest of all sounded the
footsteps of the master of the mansion pacing

up and down, as they had done the greater part of the night. Firm, hard, cruel they sounded, as the iron-heeled sandal ground on the delicate marble. Thwarted where he least expected opposition, a foe arisen at his very hearthstone, baffled in his search for Marcella, who, he rightly believed, had not only led his daughter into the company of this degraded sect, but also given her shelter when he had driven her from his doors, his savage temper was now wrought up to a pitch of fury. His features were swollen with passion, his eyes bloodshot and glaring, his whole look that of a tiger who, having once tasted blood, can find no rest until he may renew his horrible banquet. His slaves feared to approach him, they obeyed what orders he gave promptly, for he was in no mood to be further angered; but they only addressed him to bring to him from time to time the messages which arrived from the officers of the law, stating that although a few Christians had been captured, many of them, and among them those whom he most sought, had taken refuge in the catacombs, whence it would be impossible to unearth them.

The clepsydra in the fountain, as well as the sun-dial over the door, indicated near noon, when the brazen door leading from the atrium to the entrance porch was thrown open and a visitor entered.

Sergius Pollonius had just reached the upper end of the hall in his walk, and turned so as to face the intruder, and so astonished was he at the sight that he stopped short. It was the child whose acquaintance we have already made in the Via Aureum and the catacombs. Her sallow cheeks were burning with excitement. She pushed back the hair that shaded her forehead, and her black eyes seemed fairly to flash with determination. She did not pause a moment to look at what must have been a novel sight to her, she apparently had no room in her pre-occupied mind for either curiosity or fear, for she ran directly to the Roman noble, and caught him by the robe.

"Sergius Pollonius, gather your men together and come with me quickly!"

The master of the house was for a moment confounded at this strange address, but recovering himself, said sarcastically: "And who are you whom I am to have the honor of following?" Then without waiting for an answer he thundered out to his slave, "Here, Zenos, turn this beggar brat from my doors!"

The child turned pale, and stamped her foot on the ground with rage at finding herself mocked.

"Very well," she cried, "mock, if you choose, the only person who can tell you where to find what you are seeking!"

Pollonius, in his varied intercourse with the

world, had learned that it is not safe to despise even an apparently contemptible co-adjutor, and that assistance, as well as opposition, is often found in the quarter where we least expect it; so he stepped forward and grasped the child by the arm.

"If you are trifling with me, girl, it will be the worse for you. Who sent you to me?"

"No one; I would go by myself as I came by myself, if I did not want you more than you seem to want me."

"Well, what do you want?"

The Roman's tone had changed; it was still gruff and moody, but no longer disdainful. He had found that his strange visitor was too proud to care for his pride, or to fear his anger.

"I want revenge!" said the strange creature, drawing up her deformed figure to its greatest height; "I want revenge, and you can help me to it. I've got them all safe

7*

there; there is enough to feed the lions for a month!   There are two passages closed up, and you must bring soldiers enough to take them all."

"Whom do you mean?"

The child made a gesture of impatience.

"Those that you and I both hate—the Christians, the Nazarenes; they are all together at their worship, bishop and people, and a new convert with them; you can take them in the very act of breaking the edict."

"A new convert, say you?" said Pollonius, his brow darkening. "Was it a fair maiden, was it—?" He paused, he was not quite ready to proclaim his disgrace to the world.

"I know not if it were a lady or no," replied the girl carelessly. "She is fair enough, but the lions will not have *her*, *she* will recant easily enough; but there is Marcella, the vintner's daughter, she does more to spread it than all the rest put together. But if you do not haste they will be gone; they burrow like rats, in those catacombs."

Pollonius needed no urging now. Revenge stood ready for him. He already saw in imagination that noble girl, whose purity had so often shamed his foulness, who had blessed where he had cursed, and protected where he had outraged, trembling in his power. It took him but a short time to obtain a band of soldiers, who, as we have seen, led by the child, effectually barred every avenue of escape. His victims were already as safe as if immured in the dungeons of the Mamertine prison.

When the worshippers arose from their knees, and first became aware of the danger, or rather hopelessness of their situation, they expressed little astonishment, less fear; only husbands and wives gazed mutely in each other's faces, and parents gathered their children in their arms, and the younger men collected around the bishop, who had arisen and stood calmly facing his foes. Paulina gave a cry of terror and clung to her friend's waist. As for Marcella herself, there was a bright look in her eyes, and a rising color on her cheek, as she gathered her robe firmly in her right hand. Her whole attitude was that of one who has been waiting to be called, and now hears the summons. But amid all this heroism, there was infinite tenderness in the way in which she passed her left arm around the trembling girl and upheld her. It was something far different from stoicism which sustained those helpless women and men in that most trying moment. There was neither indifference nor anger in those calm faces, and the submission with which they yielded as they were bound by couples to a long rope, had in it none of that recklessness and dis-regard of life which some think necessary to martyrdom.

Never perhaps had life appeared sweeter to many of them than it did that sweet summer morning as they emerged from the musty vaults of the catacombs into the fresh air and glorious Italian sunshine. The Campagna, with its gardens and villas, lay around them, the laborers, stretched beneath the trees, were taking their noontide rest ; there were birds singing among the branches, and, sweeter than the birds, the voices of some children sounded from behind a garden wall. Everything suggested life, calm, happy, every-day life, nothing tyranny and cruelty, agony and despair, torture and death, save those two bands of unresisting captives. There were about forty of them in all, men, women, and children, divided into two companies, and closely guarded by the soldiers. Paulina was not among them. When the Christians had been first seized, her father had put her in charge of certain of his own servants, and sent her to one of his summer residences on the upper part of the Tiber. Philip, who at the first thought of danger had sprung forward to the altar to warn the assembly, and so had been found close to the bishop, was coupled with him, but Marcella, by the especial order of Pollonius, bound more carefully than the rest, walked at the head of the procession with two soldiers, alone. Her hands were fastened behind her, her hair disarranged, her face very pale, but there was a majesty in the young girl's look that all this rather increased than destroyed, and yet that majesty was blended with humility and patience, showing that it was no earthly dignity she bore so gracefully, so royally; that the crown, it seemed so fitting her noble brow should wear, was one made of no earthly gold, decked with no perishable gems. She seemed to pay little attention to what passed around her; she answered none of the questions put to her. These were indeed few; there was something about her which repelled curiosity, and even the rudest soldier would have shrunk from an insulting word or look.

As they entered the city gates the sun beat down with noontide fervor on their unprotected heads; the dust, too, as they passed through the more crowded thoroughfares, became oppressive. Philip felt the aged bishop totter at his side, and tried with some success to so place his manacled hands, that the old man might lean a little on them. He received for this attention a word of grateful thanks, but he scarcely heard it. The luxurious young Greek felt the heat and weariness of the way more, perhaps, than many of his companions, for most of them were laborers accustomed to daily toil. But he was not thinking of this at the moment; he knew well enough that one word to the centurion who walked at his side, explaining his reason for being in the catacombs, and asserting his rights as a stranger, especially if accompanied by promise of a bribe, and by references to some of his powerful friends, would set him free, but, strange to say, he did not wish to utter that word. The heat, dust, weariness, and bonds, only brought more clearly before his sight a certain way-worn, sorrow-stricken man, climbing, faintingly, the side of Calvary in the far-off Palestine. The many noises of the crowd through which he passed, turned to the shouts of a throng of scornful, malicious Jews, crying : " His blood be on us, and on our children ; crucify him !" The prison which he was approaching seemed to have written over its gloomy portals, " My peace I leave with you ;" and instead of Death, that gloomy, mysterious, horrible spectre, which had seemed too terrible a thing even to speak of, he saw an empty tomb, a risen Saviour, a heavenly mansion, a waiting friend.

They paused several times that the women and children might rest, for their guards were not wantonly cruel, and at one of these, Philip, by permission of the soldier, bought some fruit, and bestowed it on his aged companion, although he himself was fainting with thirst. It was, perhaps, the first time the luxurious young Greek had denied himself a trifling gratification for the sake of another, and the old man's thanks fell strangely on his ear.

"My son, our Master, who hath said that he who gives a cup of cold water to a disciple for his love's sake, shall not lose his reward, bless thee with eternal life. Thou art a Greek, I see by thy dress, and from Ephesus, I should judge from thy speech; how fare our brethren there?"

Philip blushed and hesitated for a moment.

"Father," he answered at last, humbly, "I

am, as you say, an Ephesian, but I knew no Christians there, and none knew me."

The bishop looked up surprised.

"Who art thou then, my son, and what dost thou here in this 'band'?"

Philip's voice trembled as he answered :

"Father, I know I am not worthy to walk here at your side. Yesterday I was a worshipper of Jupiter and his hundred fellow-gods. I saw Mount Olympus filled with deities, who, partaking of the passions of men, were the poetical representations of the attributes of some great, all-pervading and avenging Being, whom I vaguely feared and tremblingly scorned. I laid garlands on their altars, and did them honor because my ancestors had so done, but no love went with them, and my only prayer was for a long life and the forgetfulness of death and the annihilation to follow it."

"But to-day," said the bishop, solemnly,

"to-day; yesterday has passed, to-morrow may never come, what of to-day?"

The young man lifted his eyes, brimming with joyful tears.

"Ay, Father! yesterday is past and gone forever. To-day I see but one God, perfect, holy, just, and loving; filling by his majesty the dreams of the poets, by his purity the aspirations of philosophers, by his tenderness the wants of the feeble and sinning. I see a Lamb sacrificed for my sins and accepted for me, and I joy with joy unspeakable in Jesus and the resurrection!"

The old man raised with difficulty his man-acled hands, and grasped those of his young companion.

"It is God's own blessed Spirit which has given thee grace to witness so good a confes-sion. May he bestow more grace, that it may continue unto the end; that it may support thee through ignominy and suffering; that even in the pangs of death thy faith may not waver."

"Father! teach me what faith is; I am so ignorant! Yesterday, I thought myself a philosopher; to-day I find I am but a child."

"The wisdom of this world is foolishness with God," replied the bishop, tenderly. "He that would be truly wise must become as a little child, that he may be taught of God. Even Christ was buried in the grave before he arose and ascended into heaven; and so we, buried with him in baptism, rise with him into newness of life."

"But, Father, I cannot be baptized now. I must go before his judgment-seat unwashed, unblessed."

"Nay, my son, not so. There is an outer baptism of water and an inner baptism of the Spirit; the material is only a type and sign of the immaterial and essential. The outer is for men's eyes, the inner is that which Christ seeks. This is the great question, Dost thou believe in Jesus of Nazareth?"

"I am so ignorant," said Philip humbly. "I hardly know what it is to believe, I have only been taught to doubt; but I know that when I hear the name of Jesus, my soul leaps up to meet it; that before the simplicity of his words, doubts and mysteries flee like mists before the rising sun; that I would count it my highest glory to bear the sign of his shame, and that the thought of him puts in my heart a strange tenderness toward all men —even yon soldier seems like a dear brother in one common Saviour; that the only pain I feel in the prospect of a near-approaching death, is that I shall have no time to prove how I love him; to bear to men perishing, as I was, the priceless boon of eternal life!"

While thus speaking they had entered the city, and were in the midst of thronging crowds of the populace, who had already been excited against them by the artifices of their enemies, and murmurs of hatred and reproach began to be heard. There were cries of, " Away with them! To the lions! To the lions!" " It is they who have brought the sickness to Rome; cursed are the Nazarenes!" Philip heard all this, and more than once the blood mounted to his cheek at some disgraceful epithet, and he tried to move on faster, but the guards restrained him. It was their object to excite the people as much as possible without producing violence, and it was not till stones began to fly that they closed in their ranks and cut their way through, with the prisoners in the centre, turning into the Via Sacra near the Forum.

But yesterday the young Greek had walked in that building with some of the noblest of the Roman youth, with health, talents, fortune, and an honored name, to encourage him to look forward to a prosperous future; to-day

he walked past it in company with the poorest
and most despised in the land, ignominiously
chained like a common felon, with nothing in
prospect but a prison and a shameful and
cruel death. Deeply he felt the change in his
situation. It is a hard thing to bear disgrace,
even if we know it to be undeserved. Severe
physical pain is often easier to endure than
the mocking laugh of a former friend, the
scorn and contempt of those who but lately
looked upon us as equals, perhaps even considered us their superiors. Such thoughts
passed through Philip's mind in all their bitterness; but then came another. Even as
one had walked the streets of Jerusalem
loaded with the obloquy of his fellow-men, so
he now walked the streets of Rome for his
dear name's sake, following in his footsteps.
He was beginning to confess him before men,
and he had that very day heard the blessing
which is annexed to that confession. His

heart began to fill with a new and intense joy. He lifted his head, which had been hanging on his breast, tossed back the hair from his brow, trod with a firmer step the dusty pavement, and fixed a gaze so eager, so expectant, on the sky, already glowing with the glories of sunset, that they reached the prison before he perceived it; and it was only when the gates of the Mamertine clashed behind him, when the roar of the populace was hushed to a low murmur, when the confined air of the gloomy stone chamber into which he was conducted struck chilly on his fevered cheek, that he awoke from his happy dream.

The room in which all the prisoners were placed was spacious, though low, and dimly lighted by two small, barred windows. Their guards having unbound them departed, leaving them to find what rest they could on a few rough benches and bundles of straw. Even this poor accommodation was welcome to the wearied band, and the coarse food which was given them at nightfall, was gratefully received. As the shadows gathered the good bishop called all together for evening prayer. In simple, touching words, the old man commended one and all to the guardianship of a loving Father during the hours of the night, and then every voice rose with his in the evening hymn.

To Philip the words were not familiar, so that he could not join in with the others, but he drank in the meaning from their lips, and his heart sang, though his tongue was silent. Then he turned to look for Marcella. Until then he had been too much occupied to think of her. The new love which had been poured into his heart was overflowing upon his companions in faith and sufferings, and he had been busy in aiding them so far as his inexperience would allow. He had hushed a little wearied, crying child, arranged the

8

straw more comfortably for an aged woman, and chafed the numb hands of the good old bishop.

At first he did not see her. Darkness had gathered rapidly. The last sobbing child had sunk to sleep, the room was very quiet, and Philip, fearing to disturb the sleepers, paused at one of the windows. Then he felt a hand laid on his arm, and turning, met Marcella's glorious eyes gazing, filled with tremulous love, into his.

"Philip! I welcome you as a prisoner of the Lord!"

"Yes. But, O Marcella! what an unworthy one!"

"A prisoner of the Lord Jesus is a prisoner of hope. Our insufficiency is his sufficiency, his strength is made perfect in our weakness. O Philip! what could we do in this hour if we could not trust in him; if we had to look back on our own works; if the eternal life were not a gift as free as it is glorious, as certain as is the existence of God? Eternal life; incorruption for corruption; power for weakness; glory for shame; endless joy for temporal pain! Truly when this is accomplished, shall come to pass the words which were spoken—'Death shall be swallowed up in victory. O Death! where is thy sting? O grave! where is thy victory? Thanks be to God who giveth us the victory through our Lord Jesus Christ!'"

Philip had never heard these words before, but they expressed so perfectly the joy of his heart that he felt their inspiration, and turned with an exclamation of delight toward his cousin.

She was leaning against the window, her face very pale from weariness, but her eyes beaming with their strange, unearthly brilliancy, her lips parted, her hands clasped, her gaze fixed on the little spot of fading crimson sky which the prison bars had not entirely shut out, but her vision seemed to pierce far beyond that distant barrier and revel in things unutterable. It is that look which is said to belong only to the faces of those who die young, a sight which embraces more of the future than the present, more of the spiritual than of the material, more of the unseen than the seen. Philip had noticed this before, but had never understood it, it had seemed to him weird, unnatural, unearthly; he now saw that though incomprehensible to the heathen atheist, it was not so to the Christian believer. It was not of earth, but it was of heaven, heavenly. For himself the vision was not yet so clear, the illumination was not yet so bright. He watched Marcella as we watch one who, having attained the summit of a hill from which home is visible, stands rapt in the beautiful vision which only painful climbing can reveal to us.

"O Marcella! tell me, what is beyond, what do you see?"

The brightness died away from her face as the crimson had done from the sunset cloud.

"It was only for a moment," she said, so wearily, leaning her face on her clasped hands, "only a moment, but it was very beautiful. O Philip! the joy is worth the suffering, the crown many times repays the cross."

CHAPTER VIII.

Philip's Decision.

MORNING dawned over the Eternal City. The many gates were thrown open, and the peasants flocked in with their merchandise, and travellers from the ends of the world entered, wondering at every step. From the palace-crowned hills came the few nobles on their way to the luxurious bath or the exciting forum; from the valleys at their feet came forth the many laborers, mechanics, and beggars. The beggars whined for alms; the nobles contemptuously tossed them their oboli. The children played merrily in the public gardens and streets, the workman whistled at his task, the mother sang her baby to sleep, as she sat working at her window. In a word, Rome lived that day as it had lived many days before, as it hoped to live many days after, as it wished to live forever. Everything spoke of excitement, luxury, pomp, and power. A stranger would never have thought how many anxious hearts were beating in that mighty city, upon how many desolate homes that morning sun was shining.

Never had the shady lane leading to the house of Marcus the vintner, looked more inviting; never had it been more silent. The dew which lay thickly on the lawn had not been brushed aside by any intruding feet. On the steps of the porch, and on the vines which overhung it, Marcella's doves cooed in vain for their morning crumbs, and the caresses of their mistress' gentle hand. The sun, peeping through the vine-curtained windows, glanced on the smooth, unused beds, and seemed to linger wonderingly about a broken toy which lay on the floor where little hands had dropped it.   Would they ever seek it again ?   The loom stood idle against the wall, with the half-finished web in it ; but the shuttle was empty and lay on the shelf. There too lay the well-used distaff, with the hank of wool beside it.   The mother's busy fingers have done with those homely tasks ; she has other work to do for the master.

Philip's room was hardly in such order. On his table lay a roll of papyrus, on which he had commenced an epistle to his friends in Greece, and a tablet with a half-finished sketch of the temple of Apollo.   His pencils and colors lay scattered about, and behind them stood an open volume of Socrates, supported on a book-rack of sculptured bronze, representing Minerva crowning Plato with an olive chaplet, and pointing upward to where Jupiter, thunderbolt in hand, bent toward him from his throne; and Venus, forgetful of her beauty, and Atlas, of his heavy burden, seemed as if entranced with the eloquence of the favored mortal.

Let the unfinished picture and epistle lie there. They tell of a life comparatively harmless and innocent, though selfish and sadly wasted. But close the roll of Socrates, and lay aside the carved fable. Philip, in the Mamertine, has better things than these. The philosophy of the wisest of the Greeks was but as child's talk to the wisdom of the Nazarene; he had seen diviner beauty than that of Venus; he rested on the arm of a God to whom Jupiter was but as a shadow passing away.

The sun rose higher, and looked down on a fast increasing crowd in the Via Sacra. The teeming alleys of the metropolis had poured forth their thousands, until the whole of the magnificent street, from the prison to

the forum, was one great mass. They had
waited patiently for more than one weary
hour, but now a murmur arises which swells
into a shout; for see! far down the street,
the flashing of light from polished steel;
listen to the trampling of horses; see the
banners of Rome floating on the breeze; how
the golden eagles flash through the cloud of
dust! Here come the conquerors of the
world with new captives; this must be another triumph for Rome, already almost sated
with victory. But who is the first of these
captives? An aged gray-haired man. The
second? A pale, simply dressed girl. The
rest? Unarmed men, feeble women, helpless
children. Truly a noble triumph for the city
of the Cæsars to behold!

There was nothing wonderful in the sight
to make people stare so. That noble old man
had walked their streets in an innocent and
holy life for seventy years. Many of the

others were their friends, their fellow-work-
men, their neighbors, their kindred ; and yet
there was a strange fascination for the Roman
crowd in that little, helpless band of captives.
The quiet, harmless lives of the Christians
had won for them the favor of most in the
middle and lower classes ; but there had
lately broken out a strange sickness in the
city, and the party opposed to the fast-increas-
ing sect had seized upon this opportunity to
further their plans by insinuating among the
ignorant mob that all this trouble was caused
by the Christians, and that the fatal miasma
was made by them in their secret haunts
among the catacombs, and sent forth to desolate the city. There is nothing on earth so
fickle as the crowd that throngs an over-
grown city, and so it happened that hands
into which Marcella had poured her bene-
factions, were raised to point at her ; children
whom she had fondled on her knees were

lifted on their parent's shoulders to add their shrill shrieks of derision to the voices of their elders, and shake their tiny fists with the rest.

Marcella herself seemed to heed none of these things ; perhaps she did not see them. She walked forward very quietly, her eyes cast downward, her plain dress arranged with its accustomed neatness, her beautiful hair coiled in smooth braids around her shapely head. She was pale, but there was not about her that air of supernatural exaltation and abstraction, which poets and painters love to delineate in the faces of martyrs. She looked very, very like a sad and weary woman. Never had she looked more beautiful ; but it was not her beauty which hushed for an instant the tumult, and calmed the passions of that brutal crowd. It was rather the gentle dignity which was expressed in every motion of her noble figure. She seemed so like what they had daily seen walking the streets, and entering their dwellings, that they could not believe her a criminal being led before her judges. If they had realized her danger, if they had seen in those manacled hands the presage of her fearful doom, the low murmurs of "Our Marcella! Marcella of Rome!" that fell in tones of wonder, and even of affection, might have swelled to a shout which would have shaken the palaces of the Cæsars, and thousands of brawny hands might have snatched from the maiden the martyr's crown and palm, now seeming so very near. But it was not to be. The murmur died away; the guard proceeded without interruption until they entered the hall of judgment, and then, the gates being closed in the faces of the throng, they were left to await the moment when they might shout their applause at the result of the trial. If it were favorable, they would escort the released captives triumphantly to their homes; if the contrary, they could rejoice in the prospect of what they so dearly loved—a grand bloody drama in the Colosseum. It made little matter, they would have seen the show!

Within the judgment-hall all was quiet and order. The judge sat in his chair of state, the witnesses were gathered in goodly array, executioners with their instruments of torture stood on one side, and, on the other, a gayly-decked altar, and a priest with garlands ready for sacrifice—these were the alternatives to be presented to the Nazarenes.

The venerable bishop stepped forward first; he, who had so long led his little flock, would not now draw back in the hour of their fierce temptation. But before he had time to speak a word, he was pushed aside by a young girl who had been standing among the crowd gathered behind the judge's chair.

"Philip! Philip!" she said, seizing the young man's hands and trying to draw him away, "I am so glad I have found you at last! Soldiers! take off these chains; he is my brother, he has nothing to do with these Christians!"

Peremptory as was the maiden's tone, the guard was not quite ready to obey her unless backed by other authority, and looked at the judge for instructions. The judge himself seemed quite amazed.

"Who is this girl? What has she to do with the prisoner?"

"My lord," said a man, evidently a noble by his dress, who was leaning against the back of the magisterial chair, "the maiden is a Grecian from Ephesus, and that is her brother. They came here not two months ago, and are no Christians. I know their father well, Tithonius of Ephesus; the emperor has no better friend in all Greece. How the lad has fallen in with such company, I do not know, but certain I am that he has nothing to do with this disreputable sect."

The judge's brow relaxed.

"Guards, release that young man. Philip of Ephesus, for thy father's sake I will not have thee stand in such company."

The bonds fell from Philip's hands, the cord by which he was fastened to his fellow-prisoners was hastily cut, but he did not move. The judge was bending kindly toward him, the noble who had interfered in his behalf had made some steps forward to take him by the hand, but still he did not move. There was a deep silence, while every eye in the crowded judgment-hall was fastened on him ; at last he broke it :

"My lord judge, my sister and the noble Maximus mistake. I am indeed the son of Tithonius of Ephesus, and a good friend to our lord the emperor, but I am a Christian."

The judge's face darkened, and he turned

to the noble ; the latter only looked incredulous, and said sarcastically :

"There is no accounting for the whims of youth, but if you will suffer him to come aside for a moment with me, I will endeavor to ascertain the meaning of this very strange assertion."

The judge assented, and gave the necessary order, and in a few minutes Philip found himself separated from his companions and led to a large, luxuriously furnished apartment, where he was soon joined by Maximus. The latter threw himself down on a cushioned couch, and motioned Philip to an equally comfortable seat, but he declined respectfully.

"My lord, I am a prisoner ; it is not meet that I should sit in your presence."

"Philip of Ephesus!" said Maximus angrily, "for your father's sake, who has done me more than one favor, I have used my influence to protect you from the consequences of some foolish freak into which you have fallen, probably unawares ; and have brought you here to talk to you, as man to man, and save you from the disgrace to which a public trial for such a crime would subject you and your family. But I warn you that my patience has its limit, and my favors are not to be slighted ; they will not be offered twice. What did you mean by the foolish declaration you made in the hall just now ?"

"You are very kind to take this interest in me, Maximus," replied the young man quietly, "and in my father's name and my own I thank you ; but what I said just now is true ; I can only repeat it, I am a Christian."

"Do you know what that means ?" said Maximus sternly.

"Hardly," replied Philip ; "I can hardly understand it yet ; it is too grand and glorious a thing for me to comprehend so soon ;

I only know it means peace and joy and hope and love."

"All this is nonsense," said Maximus, rising angrily; "I ask you again—do you know that to be a Christian means to be an enemy to the Roman nation—Rome, that rules the world: that to be a Christian means degradation, poverty, infamy; that to be a Christian means a prison, torture, agony, death? Answer me, do you know this?"

"As to the first," replied the young man calmly, "I am no enemy to Rome. Rome has no better subjects than those she despises. As for the second, the Master I serve has borne all this for me; it cannot be shame to follow in the footsteps of a God. As for the last, to be a Christian means not death, but life—life eternal and glorious, life of soul and body."

"I do not understand you," replied Maximus. "It is as certain as that you stand there, that unless you renounce these notions, you will suffer imprisonment and torture, probably a cruel and disgraceful death. The lions in the Colosseum will soon change your ideas of death. Why, your Christ, this Nazarene, is dead; crucified like a slave a hundred years ago. What have you to do with him ? What can he do for you ?"

"He can make me stand here and listen unmoved to your threats, and he will give me strength to bear your tortures with equal composure ?"

"How long have you held these opinions ?" said Maximus, after a minute's pause.

"Since yesterday."

"Since *yesterday !*" repeated the Roman with surprise. "Why you were only arrested yesterday ?"

"It was so, my lord; when I was arrested I had hardly yet decided—that is, I had not yet understood it." For it seemed a wrong thing to the young convert to speak of *deciding* in such a matter. As if a thirsty man should speak of *deciding* whether he would drink the cool draught held to his lips; as if the fugitive, hunted to the death, should hesitate about accepting a safe refuge opened before him.

"One would hardly think," replied Maximus, "that *that* would be a circumstance calculated to influence you in the way it seems to have done. But how did you happen to be with these Christians? They do not generally admit the uninitiated into their mysteries."

"I was not with them," said Philip. "I went to seek my friends, and was wandering, lost among the catacombs, when I was met, and conducted to their place of meeting."

"And what did you see there?" exclaimed the Roman eagerly. "What were their incantations, their ceremonies?"

Philip smiled, as he thought how little these terms applied to the simple worship which he had witnessed.

"I did not see any incantations. They offered up prayers and thanksgivings, and listened to words from their holy books."

"To whom did they offer these prayers and thanksgivings?"

"To God, and Christ as God," replied Philip, reverently.

"To God!" replied the Roman, peevishly. "To which God? There are enough of them, I trow. See the arrogance of these fellows. We offered to place a statue of their god in the Pantheon, with all the rest, but, by Jupiter! they thought the Pantheon itself was not large enough to hold him, or else he was too fine for the company of Mount Olympus, for they must needs turn the father of the gods himself from his throne to make a fitting place for the crucified Nazarene. Ah! young man, moderation is a great thing. You Christians must have all, so you get nothing."

"Maximus," said Philip, firmly, looking him full in the face, "if the emperor were to find his throne occupied by the offscouring of Rome, do you think he would be content to sit down amongst them, an equal?"

"Hardly," replied Maximus, his lip curling with scorn. "But," he continued angrily, as Philip had expected, "young man do you know that you have insulted the gods of your ancestors by that speech?"

"Who was Mercury," replied Philip, undaunted, "but the god of thieves and liars? Who was Venus, but an abandoned woman? Who is Juno, but personified hatred and jealousy? Who is Bacchus, but an embodiment of lust, greed, and sensuality? Truly, I might go through the whole list and scarcely find one whom an honest Roman matron would admit into her house, were they men and women. And who is Jupiter himself, that he cannot rule his own court of gods and demi-gods, who rage and quarrel among themselves, more like a set of foolish children than superhuman minds. Such are thy deities, O Rome!"

"And what is your God?" asked Maximus, repressing his anger with an effort.

Philip closed his eyes, and clasped his hands, as if collecting all his mental powers for the answer.

"My God is a being of infinite power, controling by his word the universe and all it contains. He is a being of perfect justice, swayed by no passions, biassed by no prejudices. He is a being of infinite wisdom, comprehending as one the past, the present, and the future. He is a being of infinite, unfathomable, incomprehensible love; love exercised not merely generally over his creation, but individually to each one of his created beings;

love protecting, consoling, supporting, redeeming, sympathizing; love which stooped to incarnate itself for the redemption of those who despised and rejected it; love that bestowed on those who sought its death the priceless boon of immortality."

There was silence for a few moments, broken at last by Maximus.

"Time is passing. Philip of Ephesus, we being here alone, I am free to confess to you that I think but little better of our gods than you do, and I know that nine-tenths of those who think on the subject at all would say the same; but, as for this other being—" he paused and his voice trembled when he resumed—"it sounds more like a dream of Plato than anything that could possibly be. If there were really such a being—but, nonsense! should that which Plato failed to discover be revealed to fishermen and carpenters? Time passes, as I said before. Hold

9

what opinions you please of the deities, but submit so far to custom and prejudice as to offer them the customary honors, which, after all, are nothing. Look at that clepsydra in the fountain. Keep silent, think and decide. When there have dropped three blue pebbles I will hear your decision, and it must be a final one. Do not throw away youth, talents, riches, honors, and fame at one cast of the die."

Philip only bowed in response, and there was silence, broken only by the silvery plash of the fountain, and the singing of birds in the garden below. At length the third blue pebble fell in its marble basin, and the startled goldfish swam away from the tiny waves it produced.

"Philip," said the Roman kindly, "I have been thinking how you might rise in the emperor's senate, with such a gift of oratory as you possess. Tell me your thoughts."

The young man lifted his eyes, brimming with tears, and gazed into the Roman's face, with a look so full of joy and peace, that the latter waited in anxious wonder for the words which would follow.

"Maximus, I was thinking of eternal life."

CHAPTER IX.

Cross instead of Crown.

THE setting sun found the Christians again in their prison, with new additions to their numbers; but when the evening hymn was raised, few voices, and those weak and quivering ones, joined in the strain. Torture, in all its possible forms, had done its work; neither age nor sex had been spared, and some, considered as the principal offenders, had been removed to separate cells. Mothers sat weeping for the little ones whom they had seen snatched from their arms, and either murdered before their eyes or sold as slaves. There were low moans of anguish from those whose twisted limbs and burnt and mangled flesh bore witness to the fiery trial to which their faith had been subjected ; but as one of the ministers, for the aged bishop was lying exhausted on his pallet, led their devotions, he gave thanks that not one of their number had wavered in the faith, and that the good Shepherd, who had that day taken into his arms so many of the lambs of the flock, had made true the words of Scripture, that "out of the mouth of babes and sucklings God had perfected praise."   Philip, who by the interference of Maximus had been spared the torture, passed from one to another, binding up wounds and bestowing freely all he had to give—tenderness and sympathy. It was a new situation for him ; but the overflowing joy in his heart made it easy for him to bestow of his abundance on those around him. Unaccustomed as was the young patrician to such labors, his high breeding itself gave him that tact and insight into character which led him to adapt his words and deeds to the various necessities of those around him; and many were the words of thanks and blessing which made the blood mount into his cheek, partly from pleasure, partly from shame at the long years wasted in selfishness and indolence. And how few days or even hours now remained in which to atone for a wasted life! Christ's blood had atoned for all sin, he knew that; but he longed to do something for this newly found Lord. Never had life appeared so valuable to him as now, when it seemed so nearly finished. When he thought of the millions who knew nothing of this glorious news, of this heavenly gospel, who were dying without a knowledge of the life that lay within their grasp, and especially when he thought of his parents still in darkness, and Eudora left alone in the great city, he felt as if he could not die, that God would grant him a few more years, of which he would not waste a single moment, but would go about from one end of the world to the other proclaiming the great gifts of God—his Son, and everlasting life. Yet, as he looked at the stone walls and grated windows of his prison, he felt that it would be much wiser to give his thoughts to that far more probable event, a speedy death, and it was with the words on his lips, "Be thou glorified in thy own way, my Saviour," that he fell asleep.

The Christians fully expected to be led to their martyrdom the next day, but such was not the case. The emperor's birthday was approaching, and great were the preparations for its celebration. Three-decked triremes, manned by trained Numidian rowers, were to have mock combats in the Naumachiæ, or great artificial ponds constructed for the purpose. There were to be triumphal processions in the Via Sacra, reviews on the field of Mars, and the imperial gardens were to be thrown open to the public, and illumined at night by thousands. of colored lanterns. But all agreed that the spectacles in the Colosseum would be the grandest of all. Thracian peasants, torn from their native wilds and carefully instructed in the "noble art of self-defence," would be brought into the arena to fight with each other until one was slain, when the survivor might look around and see how the noble Romans, whom he had amused by his agonies, held their thumbs. If the majority of these perfumed members were held erect, he might hope to enjoy a few days of ease to recruit his bruised and battered body before entering anew into the combat, or even, if he had been remarkably successful, to receive his liberty; but woe to him if his sinew limbs had failed him or his eye had not been quick enough to please the fastidious critics, already *blasés* with horrors; down went the tips of the merciless judges, and the miserable, panting wretch, giving one thought perhaps to the blue hills of his native land, and his little sister playing at his mother's side in their rude cottage home, laid down his head upon the gory sands, and, when the blue sky had grown black to his glazed eye, and the shouts and hisses of those he had failed sufficiently to please had become dull to his deadened ear, he was dragged forth to be flung into the Tiber, to float, a swollen, hideous thing, down its turbid waters to the ocean.

But there was still another entertainment to be offered to the emperor, nobles, and such of the people as could find places on the spacious benches of the Colosseum. The King of Numidia had lately sent, as a gift to the emperor, some fine Numidian lions, and these noble beasts were to be publicly fed, after fasting a few days to whet their appetites, on

9*

the flesh of men, women, and children, con-
victed of the crime of having failed in paying
due respect to the will of the conquerors of
the world. This group, withdrawn, not only
by their guilt, but by their social position,
utterly beyond the sphere of a noble Roman's
sympathy, would be placed, defenceless, in
the midst of the arena, and then, when the
spectators had sufficiently enjoyed the pleasures of anticipation, a roar like a dozen thunders would be heard, and as the massive iron
gates opened at the emperor's signal, the
kings of the African forest would rush forth,
and soon, amid the plaudits of the whole
throng, whose shouts, rending the sky, will
drown the death-shrieks of the victims, there
will be nothing left but gore and bones and
the fierce beasts, with their glaring eyes and
tangled manes and blood-stained mouths and
paws. Then, when there would be no hope
of any further excitement, the slaves would

drive back the satiated beasts to their dens, the multitudes would disperse ; the nobles to rest, after their exertions, on the couches of their banqueting-halls, and sip the fiery Falernian to whet their jaded appetites for the cœna ; the lower classes to recount to their wives and children over their simpler meal the events of the day. And the stars would come out, calm and still, and gaze down into the now silent arena, and the moon would throw the long, ghastly shadows of the arches across the trodden sands, and the only living beings in that so lately crowded building would be spectre-like figures gliding through the galleries and out into the silvery light. Women there would be, poor, crouching, trembling creatures, bearing white cloths and small bottles, and then, starting at every sound—even at the breeze moaning among the pillars—they would gather up reverently, gently, tearfully, the scattered, half-gnawed bones, and wrap them in the cloths, and fill the bottles with the blood that lay in little horrid pools on the sand ; and then, fearfully, silently as they came, they would steal away with their treasures—whither? Few knew, fewer cared; but He, in whose sight the blood of his martyrs is very precious, will know where the holy relics are hidden, and will have them in his safe keeping until his appointed resurrection day.

Meanwhile the prisoners, although carefully guarded, were allowed a certain amount of liberty. Some of the most insignificant were after a few days liberated, and others from time to time were added to their number. They held their assemblies for worship undisturbed in the large prison room, and at one of those, clothed in a pure white robe according to the beautiful custom of these early Christians, Philip received the rite of baptism. According to these same customs, white must be the dress of the new convert for six weeks after the sacrament was received, and the young Greek felt that, before that time should have passed, they would no doubt be exchanged for those spotless garments which they wear who walk, ever free, the golden streets of the Celestial City. And this thought gave him increasing joy, for though he longed no less to spread abroad the sweet message of peace, yet he grew less confident of himself. He saw that all evil was not yet conquered in him; that the cross, so lately marked upon his forehead, was to be, if he stayed in the world, a sign of fierce conflict, and he longed for the rest, the purity, the perfection of heaven.

As he was standing one day by the window of the prison, absorbed in these thoughts, there was a little confusion in the corridor, and the door of the room was unbolted and thrown open, but he knew nothing of it till a heavy hand was laid on his shoulder, and the voice of the chief jailer said, " Is this he whom you seek, noble sir?"   And turning, he beheld his father whom he had left in Ephesus, the judge who had condemned him, and Maximus who had interfered in his behalf.

Philip looked into the face of Tithonius of Ephesus with wonder and grief, for it was not a pleasant face to look upon and call it father. The last time he had seen him was when the Tyrian galley was leaving the coast and Philip was surrounded by young men from his gymnasium, who had gathered to witness the departure of one who had been the most distinguished of their number, and to whom they shouted prophecies of new laurels to be gath ered in the great West.   Then that face had been flushed with joy and pride, overcoming even the pain of parting as he bade him bring back to his ancestors' halls the honors and fame which the gods would no doubt bestow on one so worthy of their patronage. And to the youth thus leaving his native shores, it seemed as if this adulation were but the first faint whispers of the glory which the whole world might one day lay at his feet.

And now father and son stood once more face to face in the dungeon of the Mamertine. On the brow of the one, instead of the anticipated laurels, rested ignominy and public disgrace; and on the father's face, instead of pride and love, was indignation mingled with overwhelming shame. He stood a little behind the rest, his hands folded in his mantle, his brow contracted, his cheeks pale, his mouth firmly set. He remained perfectly silent, and the jailor repeated his question, at the same time touching the young man on the shoulder:

"Is this the one you seek, Tithonius of Ephesus?"

The father started, and for a reply only

repeated the words, "Is this the one you seek, Tithonius of Ephesus?" in a tone so bitter that Maximus interfered.

"Nay, Tithonius, you promised to deal gently with the youth; he is your son after all."

"*Is* this my son that I sent forth from my home three months ago?" repeated the Greek still more harshly.

Philip could bear it no longer, and sprang forward. "Yes, father! I *am* your son, your only son. Do not look so—do not speak so; let me have your blessing before I die!"

"My blessing on a felon!" replied Tithonius. "Blessings on a son who has disgraced a spotless name! *My* son in a felon's cell, condemned to die a slave's death!"

"Yet not from any fault of mine," exclaimed Philip, eagerly yet humbly, "none can say that; and this is everlasting life that

I have found here, and it is glory and joy that await me, not shame!"

"Is this a madman you have brought me to see?" said the Greek, unmoved, as he repulsed his son's offered embrace, and turned to the judge.

"As for his crimes," was the answer, "they are not probably very serious, for these Christians are, whatever else may be said of them, pure enough in their lives to put us to the blush. It is not so much that he has done evil as that he refuses to do a very simple thing which the emperor has commanded, saying that he cannot believe in the gods or even reverence them."

"Who asks him to believe in them," said Maximus, pettishly breaking into the conversation, "or who asks him to reverence them either? For my part, if reverencing all the deities that occupy places in the Pantheon were a test, I might as well take my place here at once and fatten for the lions. Believe in fifty thousand gods or none, just as you please; after all, it is only a question of custom. I lay a garment on an altar occasionally, and swear by Jupiter and Bacchus, and then enjoy my baths and wine with the rest, thinking of the gods what I please."

"And the hereafter, Maximus," said Philip, turning full upon him, "the eternal life, what of that?"

The Roman's cheek flushed, and then he sighed: "Ah! that is a beautiful dream—if it were true—but—"

Here the judge interrupted.

"Enough, young man," he said, sternly. "Do not seek to spread your madness any further. You are fortunate in having powerful friends willing to consider this affair as one of the follies of youth, not to be too severely dealt with. So the emperor has granted to the prayers of his good friend and subject,

Tithonius of Ephesus, the life of you, his son, on condition that within ten days you leave Italy, never to enter its boundaries again." Then, as Philip stood perfectly still, as if stunned by this sudden change in his fortunes, he continued: "Come, young man, one would think you had been near enough death to make this news better than it seems at first." Then he added still more kindly, laying his hand on his arm as he saw the youth's bewildered expression: "Come with us to my bath near by, and lay aside these prison garments, and you will feel that you are really free."

Philip seemed only to catch at the word "robe," and, drawing his white garment closer around him, murmured incoherently: "My robe! It is my baptismal robe; I must not soil it; it must be kept pure; only a few days, and then my crown and palm. Must I go away? I would rather not; I thought it was all over. The eternal life, I would rather have that?"

He seemed so distressed and confused, as he turned from one to another, that even his father's face softened a little, and Maximus, who had a kind heart beneath his apparent carelessness, drew Philip's arm within his own, and tried to turn him away.

"Come out of this dungeon! This place is enough to turn the head of any one. My lord judge, we can settle this matter much better at my baths than here."

And so, hardly conscious where he was going, the young Greek found himself led out into the pure air under the glorious Italian sky. Once he paused in the corridor leading to the part of the prison where Marcella was confined, and wished to speak with her; but neither the judge nor his father would permit it, and so it came to pass that he and his cousin never met on this earth again.

CHAPTER X.

Crown instead of Cross.

ALL Rome was astir when as yet the sun had hardly peeped over the distant Apennines. In the cool of the morning the peasants from the neighboring country came thronging along the various roads. The fishermen of Ostia and Portus left their nets, the farmers of the Campagna their half-cut corn, the vine-dressers their ungathered grapes, and turned their steps toward a common centre. The shop-keepers, except such as dealt in the fruits and drinks which the thirsty multitude would be sure to want before the day was over, closed their shops, and, dressed in holiday attire, with their wives and children, went out into the streets and public squares. Even the indolent Roman noble awoke with feelings of unusual interest in the entertainment this day was to afford him.

There was not a cloud in the heavens. The rising sun looked down from the glorious Italian sky upon a land dressed in its gala robes. The city lay spread beneath it with its streets of stately houses and temples, its glittering palaces, the soft, green expanses of the public parks, the sparkling spray of countless fountains; even sluggish old father Tiber seemed to toss gold about on the peaks of his tiny waves. Farther on, the long sweep of golden grain fields on the Campagna melted on the one side into the misty blue of the distant Apennines, and on the other into the deeper azure of the Mediterranean. But in order to have comprehended the full beauty of this magnificent scene, we should have been elevated far above it both in body and mind, and this certainly no Roman was that day. It mattered little to him that earth and sky were alike radiant in beauty, except as it promised him that he should not be interrupted in his sport by unfavorable weather, for it was the birthday of the emperor of all the Roman world, and all the Roman world would keep high holiday.

Already the grand triumphal procession is forming in the Campus Martius, and the swelling burst of trumpets in the distance announces that the emperor is about to set forth in his chariot to take his place at the head of it. Now it passes in its majestic slowness along the principal streets, pausing at the column which has just been erected in commemoration of victories in the East. There orations are made in which the conqueror and the gods are mentioned in the same breath and with equal honors. This over, they proceed to that wonder of the world, the stupendous Colosseum. There, on those elevated seats stretching up, tier upon tier, until the eye wearies of the sight, is room for ninety thousand human beings, and ten or twenty thousand more may find standing room on the stairs and in the galleries ; and now all seem full. From the golden canopied throne of the emperor to the stone seats of the plebeians far above his head, all are occupied by an eager, tumultuous throng, ready to applaud or hiss, as their fickle fancy may lead, what is enacted on the smooth expanse of white sand below them.

The games have begun. First come chariot races ; the gaily painted vehicles rush around the course, and the victor is crowned with a jewelled wreath by the emperor's own hand. The wrecks of several chariots dashed to pieces in the contest are removed and other actors appear. Gladiators contend singly and in troupes, and there begin to appear on the white sand horrid-looking spots of a dark red hue; and there are ghastly looking bodies carried out under the arches, and those in the lower tiers hear shrieks of agony and dying groans.

The excitement grows more and more intense, and as pageant follows pageant, symptoms of impatience begin to be manifested by the crowd. There are murmurs, growing louder and louder until they form themselves into words:

" The Christians! The lions! Bring them out; let us see the Christians! Long live the emperor; down with the Christians!"

The emperor rises, smiles, and makes a signal with his hand. There is an instant hush, in which the great iron doors below are heard turning on their hinges.

The early beams of that day's sun stole softly through the window of the room in the Mamertine prison in which Marcella lay asleep. She had meant to be up before the sun, in order not to lose a moment of the few last hours of her life on earth. But the night before she had been much wearied. There had been many sad leave-takings, many sad hearts to comfort, many strengthening words to say, and they all came to Marcella. She who had been the sunshine of so many souls in happier days, shone none the less brightly upon them, now that they had entered into the shadow of death. Seeming never to think of herself and her own approaching agony, she went from one to another, always ready with her words and looks of tender love and wise sympathy, as though she alone of all that company had nothing to dread. But at last the night came. For the last time they gathered together for their evening worship; for the last time the prison walls resounded with their sweet chants and hymns. They would sing them far more sweetly the next day, the bishop told them, with no sobs mingled with their tones.

And then gradually all became hushed and still, and Marcella's work was done; yes, done for ever in this world. So very young, in the very prime of youth and health and 'strength, her work was finished. No more walks in the Via Aurea among the cottages of the sburri and fossi, or talks with the fishermen mending their nets at the Ostian port. And so, her head leaning against the bars of the window, her hands clasped, hanging listless, her eyes looking up into the depths of the Italian midnight sky, she passed her whole life in review. Not so much the great events—there were very few of those—but the smaller ones. It was strange how they came trooping up, those memories of childish scenes and the trivial round of daily life. She thought of her plays with her brother and Philip up and down the vineyard walks in the dear old home.   She saw the rich, ripe clusters which her brother loved to hold just beyond her grasp, and smelled the faint, sweet perfume of the roses with which they had pelted each other till the path was covered with the delicate pink and white petals. She even remembered a little wooden horse, her first possession, and the tears she had shed when it was broken.   Somehow the painful thoughts connected with her brother's death did not come to her so freely; she rather thought of the soft, warm kisses of the little ones who had come afterward, baby lips that she had taught to smile, tiny feet whose pattering she seemed to hear coming down the garden walk to meet her at the gate.   And then all her little household duties and pleasures; there was the unfinished web in the loom, and the vine by the porch needed trimming and training, and she would like to have given a handful more of crumbs to the doves at her window. The moon was shining in at that window now, on the little white bed in which she had slept since childhood, when she used to wake in the night and be half frightened, half pleased, to see that great bright face looking into her eyes ; and as she thought of the strange fancies that ran in her childish head, she first smiled and then laughed—a little, low, childish laugh, such a laugh as she had not laughed for years, and then started to find herself in prison.

It was hard, hard even then to realize the truth. There was her home with the vine-bordered walks, the little moonlit room, the cooing doves, but nevermore for her. She had seen them for the last, last time. Other hands would train the vines and finish the web and feed the birds ; other children would play in the garden, other baby voices sound in the house, other children lie in the little white bed and dream strange, childish dreams, but she never again. She felt no pain, no weakness, no wasting of sickness ; her pulse beat with full life, her brain was clear and active, her system, which had long enjoyed, perhaps through the wonderful calmness of her mind, uninterrupted health, gave no symptom of decay of the vital powers, and yet death stood at her side. The glorious moon and stars now sweeping through the cloudless sky would come forth the next night in all their beauty, but she would never see them again ; she was gazing on their glories for the last time. Her simple, quiet life was ended, her work done.

And with this thought came a strangely mingled feeling of weariness and peace. Now that the burden was laid aside, she began to feel how heavy it had been, and to turn to the rest now so near at hand. Only a few more steps in the road, and the glorious city would be reached ; only a few short hours of suspense, one moment of pain, and then—the boundless future, the presence of God, the everlasting life !

The moon was setting behind the prison towers, and her mother touched her and interrupted these thoughts. That simple-hearted woman seldom interfered with her gifted daughter or sought to fathom the deep thoughts of her mind, but to-night she forgot all this. She only thought of her as the little one she had nursed on her knees.

"Come, Marcella, my darling, you will need your strength ; come and sleep once more at your mother's side."

"Yes, mother, I will come," she said very gently, but very wearily, "only one moment more."

She only stayed to press her face close, close against the iron bars, to feel once more the cool night breeze sweeping down from the Apennines, then she laid her head on her mother's bosom and slept like a little tired child.

There came no strong, God-sent angel to make the warders sleep and open wide the prison doors. Such was not God's will. So soundly she slept that she was only aroused by the sun falling full on her face, to find her mother sitting by her, smoothing back her hair from her face, and crooning over her a little baby-song which she had used to lull her to sleep with long years before. When the jailers came soon after to lead them forth, they found her quite ready. She was dressed with even more than her usual neatness in the simple garb she had been accustomed to wear; her hair braided back in heavy silken bands around the graceful head, her glorious eyes looking out from under their long, dark lashes as calm and steadfast as ever. There might have been a little less color than usual in her cheeks, and a slight quiver in the beautiful mouth, as she held out her hands to be bound with such meek submission that even the hardened soldier felt a strange moisture in his eyes, and turned them away from those which so patiently, so gently, gazed into his.

At length the procession was formed, the great prison gates were thrown open, and Marcella walked for the last time the familiar streets. So very familiar they seemed! She was trying to fix her thoughts on other things, but she seemed to have lost her usual calm control over them ; they would turn back to the simple trifles of her daily life. The ships seemed just as they always had seemed, and there were the statues and columns by which she had measured her way in her daily walks ; she knew just how their shadows fell at this hour in the morning ; and there was the rain-bow which she had so often watched, formed by the spray of the fountain ; and there were the boys at play in the forum. She knew

10*

even the little uneven places in the pavement over which she walked; and there, that was the corner which she always turned in going home. She would like to go home now; she would like to feel as if these last weeks had been only a strange, sad dream. Could it be possible! What was it that made this barrier between her and all this?

She lifted her eyes. Only a sea of faces— eager, gaping, curious faces—not one of which had a look of sympathy for her, faces on which her gentle ministrations had called up the smile of joy and consolation—looked upon her, in this her hour of deep anguish, hard, cold, pitiless. Having walked so long in her Master's footsteps, she walked in them to the end.

At last the short journey was ended. In one of the cavernous arches under the seats of the Colosseum they were placed to await the appointed moment when, at the emperor's command, the iron doors which alone separated them from the scene of their suffering, should open and usher them into eternity.

Marcella seated herself on a block of stone, and leaned her face upon her hands, her strength seemed to have failed her so of late. Her chains had been removed. By a refinement of cruelty, the condemned were to be allowed to use those weapons nature gave them against their fierce enemies. If, moved by natural impulses, the stronger men should madly attempt to ward off the horrid doom from the aged and the women, or if a mother, clasping her child to her, should run shrieking across the sands in the vain attempt to escape the infuriated beast bounding on her track, so much the better; it would cause a laugh of horrid derision among the spectators at such useless struggles, the sport would be so much the more worth witnessing. It was a strange scene—those gloomy vaults—that waiting company. Daylight was entirely excluded. Above their heads, lost in the darkness, rose the mighty arches which sustained the tiers of seats, massive pillars measured off the distance, and iron doors shut them in from the old familiar world on the one side, and from the unknown future before them on the other. Sometimes through those long winding cavernous passages came a deep, dull sound which made the guards clasp tighter their weapons, and more than one of the captives shrink and tremble. The lions, as well as the people of Rome, were impatient for the preliminary shows to be over. that they might enter on one more interesting to them. So it was when the hush came, and the emperor rose and waved his hand.

Back rolled the great iron doors, a flood of hot, garish daylight poured in. The prisoners were soon gathered into a group, surrounded by their guards, and led forth into the arena.   The old bishop claimed the first place.

"Let me lead my children to the very end," said he; and it was his feeble voice that began the noble chant which in a few moments rang out in clear, full harmony—children's lispings, women's trembling tones, strong men's deep, rich notes:

"We praise thee, O God! We acknowledge thee to be the Lord!"*

Marcella walked, as she had so often walked before, with two little children clinging to her, frightened at the strange scene, yet not comprehending its dreadful meaning; they buried their faces in her robe and sobbed aloud.

"Look up, little Lucian," she said once.

---

* The introduction of the Te Deum at this period is a slight anachronism, but, as the spirit of that noble hymn had long pervaded the Christian Church, and as its date is not exactly fixed, I trust I may be pardoned for placing it in the mouths of these martyrs, especially as the early writers inform us that they always went to their death as to a festival, singing hymns to their God, and to Christ as God.   F. E.

" Look up! look not around. Look up, and thou shalt see the angels !"

One of the soldiers—his great, rough heart moved to pity—took a little babe from its mother, and hid it under his cloak, saying with an oath that it should share his children's bread, and the judges be none the wiser; and the mother's tearful thanks made him add gruffly, to hide his emotion, that the next time they fed the lions he would be the meat rather than the feeder.

" To thee, cherubim and seraphim, continually do cry, Holy, holy, holy Lord God of Sabaoth ! Heaven and earth are full of the majesty of thy glory !"

Marcella moved forward in her usual calm, graceful way. For a moment she shaded her eyes with her hand from the sudden brilliant light, but when she let it fall, it rested on the head of her little brother, and remained there.

" The noble army of martyrs praise thee !"

It seemed such a long, long distance ! As if they never would come to the centre of that vast space. She seemed neither to see nor to hear. The peace and strength she had longed for had come at the last. With her eyes filled with a deeper, more heavenly expression than they had ever borne before, raised and fixed on the fathomless depths of the azure sky, she stood in the simple unaffected attitude of one waiting, but of one who has waited long and is very weary.

" The Father of an infinite majesty !"

She did not hear the murmur which succeeded the awful silence of their entrance. She did not see that the plebeians sitting on the highest seats had risen and were leaning over ; and some of them, smitten too late with a sense of their ingratitude, raised the cry, first in low tones, then in shouts :

furious with disappoi...

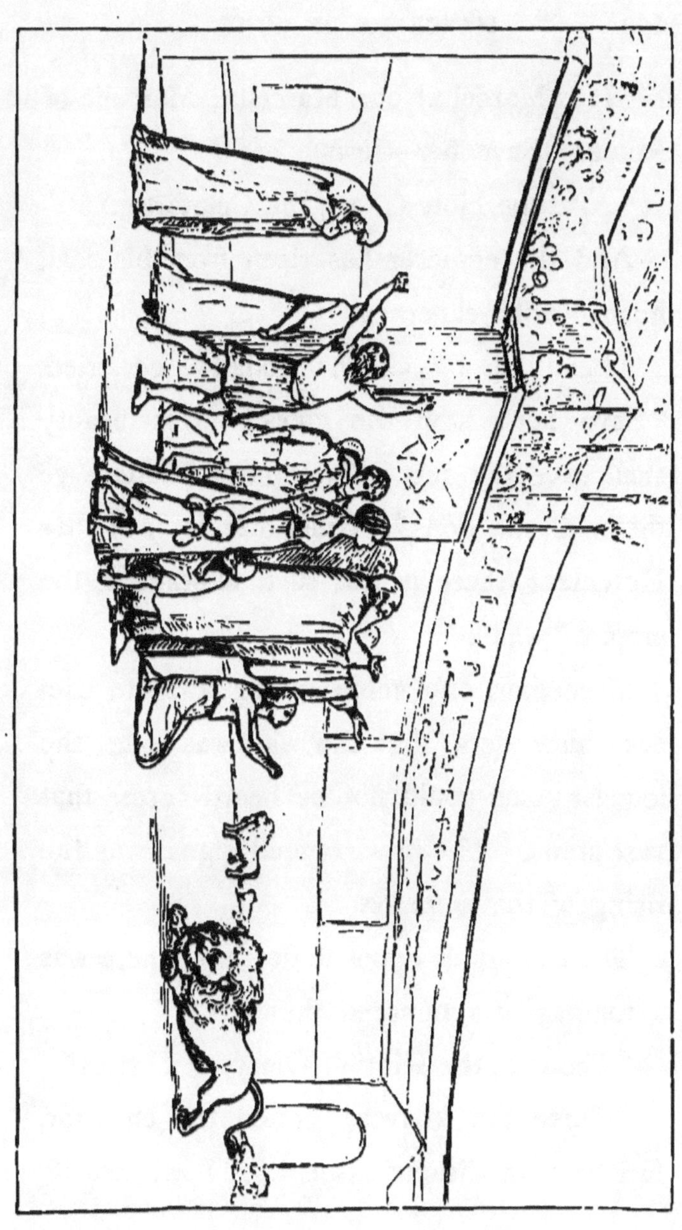

"It is Marcella! our Marcella! Marcella of Rome! Save her—rescue her!"

"Also the Holy Ghost, the Comforter."

And the emperor has risen from his seat, flushed with eagerness.

"Beautiful, by all the gods!" he cried. "Save her! stop the gates! Her beauty shall save the rest. Is it such maidens ye throw to the lions? Bring her to me! By Hercules! there is not such another in the empire."

More than one noble sprang away to execute his orders; but the way was long, the loudest voice could not be heard across that vast arena. The pre-arranged signal was the rising of the emperor.

The iron gates opposite flew up—there was a roar as of a hundred thunders.

"Thou art the King of Glory, O Christ!"

"Curse the knaves!" cried the emperor, furious with disappointment. "I will crucify

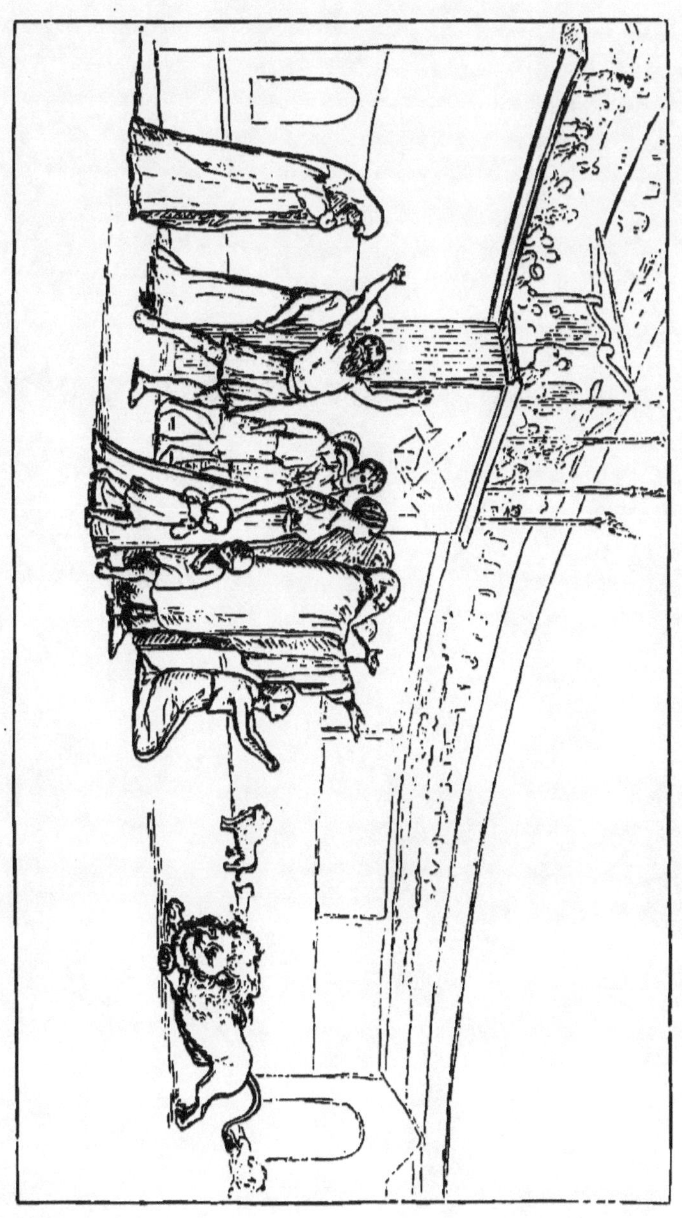

them, every one.   A thousand pounds to him who brings her to me safe!"

The gates below burst open, and forth rode twenty horsemen, urging on their steeds by whip and spur toward the group in the midst of the white sand.   But from the other side came the kings of the Numidian forest, lashing their sides with their tufted tails, glaring with red, savage eyes, bounding forward with huge, cat-like leaps straight upon their defenceless prey.

There were shouts from all parts of the amphitheatre, women shrieked and swooned, some of the men shouted to the soldiers to hasten, others to the Christians to fly, others, grown suddenly tender-hearted, hid their faces in their mantles and were silent.

"When thou didst overcome the sharpness of death, thou didst open the kingdom of heaven' to all believers."

It was really only a few moments, though

it seemed ages, and then they all knew that the lions were the victors in the race ; even as the soldiers approached, they sprang with one exultant roar into the midst of the group. But they had not only unarmed Christians to contend with ; the soldiers were among them in a moment, shouting, pricking at them with their long spears, thrusting fire-brands in their faces, until at last they turned, cowed, beaten from the remnants of their feast, and fled to their dens.

This done, and the iron gates closed upon them, the soldiers, dismounting, formed a circle around the confused mass lying on the sands. Presently the centurion remounted and rode toward the emperor, who bent eagerly down over the parapet to hear his report ; the nobles forgetful of etiquette, pressed on him, almost leaning on his shoulders.

"We have saved but three men, four women, and a child unhurt, my lord."

"But the maiden," said the emperor, "what of the maiden? She was one of the women."

"Nay, my lord," said the man, lowering his voice. "She was in the centre, and they leaped there first."

CHAPTER XI.

"Until the Morning."

THE emperor left the Colosseum with a lowering brow, and straightway a cloud seemed to fall on the whole city. The great building was deserted in almost perfect silence. The crowd in the streets did not cheer the imperial *cortége* or the chariots of the favorite nobles. Silently, sullenly they streamed along the various avenues toward their homes; but at sunset there were little groups of men at the corners of the streets, and in the fori, eagerly reading the notices which had been but just posted there. They were copies of an edict, signed by the emperor, declaring the persecution at an end. Exiles were to return, prisoners to be released, property restored, and all citizens were warned that any one maltreating a Christian would be subject to the severest penalties of the law.

The news was received in very different ways. Some laughed, shrugged their shoulders, and spoke of changeable minds; others seemed angry and uneasy; some wept like children for joy.

And so ended those days of fierce trial, and fearful agony, and terrible death. They had gone upwards to render in the account of the deeds they had witnessed to the Judge of judges. And what a record! Did the emperor imagine that by his late repentance he had entirely effaced his crime from the memory of God and man? Did he imagine that in blotting out his cruel law from the statute-book he could erase its horrid effects from the hearts of his subjects?

In the city of Rome that night there were hundreds of homes desolated. There were children crying piteously for their parents, and parents refusing to be comforted for their children ; widows in the first crushing agony of their bereavement; strong men sitting alone in the bitterness of grief over the dead ashes of their family hearths. In some cases, death seemed to have been more merciful— the whole household had gone together. In the quiet street of the vineyards the house of Marcus the vintner remained darkened, the dust lay thick on the threshold, and the doves had forsaken the window. Think of it—picture to yourself some happy family that you know, father, mother, little ones, all bound together by those subtile, yet powerful ties, various in name, but all springing from one source that makes up what we call family affections. Think of all the little daily cares lightened and brightened by being mutually shared; the little household duties, plans, projects and hopes for the future—memories sad or joyful, yet equally precious, of the past —think of all the nameless trifles which go to make up an idea of a home, and then imagine such a home struck out of the world of living beings in a moment, by the will, and for the pleasure, of one cruel, thoughtless man!

Fire and sword, torture and imprisonment, the waves of the Tiber as well as the lions in the Colosseum, had done their appointed work; but of all the souls that had gone up from that furnace of affliction to the great company of the redeemed in glory, none more noble, more saint-like, bore the palm of martyrdom than Marcella of Rome. She lay wrapped in a soldier's cloak, on a stone bench in the same arched vestibule from which she had gone forth to her death. She was in no way disfigured; the blow had come from be-

hind ; it may have been that in her rapt contemplation of the glorious future she found
it present without being conscious of the
exact moment which made the great change.
The soldiers, rough, rude men as they were,
moved so quietly around her, touched her so
gently with their clumsy fingers !   One of
them had brought a flower, a little common
flower which grew among the stones, and laid
it by her.   But they all turned aside respectfully at the sight of a group approaching.   It
was Philip, his father, and Maximus.

The young Greek seemed to have grown
years older in these few terrible days.   There
were lines of thought on his face, and his very
step had lost its lightness.   A very different
man was he from the youth who, only three
short months before, in the bright days of
early summer, had met Marcella under the
vine branches, and had been so angered with
her for being a Christian.   He had learned

many things in those three months, many more in the last three days. He had made his first acquaintance with sorrow, and it was well that he had learned where to seek for comfort. On earth he could find none. His father harsh, severe, estranged; his sister Eudora kept apart from him; those around him seeking to divert him from his painful thoughts by laughter and joking, games, shows, and trivial conversation—all seeming so very trivial to him compared with the sad realities in which he had so lately taken part. Their attempts at consolation were kind, and more than once he gratefully expressed his thanks to Maximus for his efforts to please him; but it seemed more like a bitter mockery of his sufferings.

All that fearful day he had wandered about the house, longing, oh, so earnestly! to be one of the band that he had seen passing along the street, and then waited in torturing anxiety to hear the roar and shout which would announce the accomplishment of the tragedy. It seemed to him as if the suffering of standing in the arena and watching the bounding forward of the savage beasts, and the grip of teeth and claws in shrinking flesh, would be nothing in comparison with the anguish he endured while sitting in that luxurious palace and thinking of Marcella in the Colosseum. He was sitting thus, almost stupefied with grief, when a hand touched him kindly, and he lifted up his haggard face toward Maximus.

"Why did you take me away? Why did you not let me die with her?"

"Philip!" said Maximus gravely, "your God has wrought a miracle."

Philip started to his feet, but a detaining hand was laid on his arm.

"Not as you imagine, my poor boy; the sacrifice has been accomplished, but the tide has turned. You are as free to walk the streets of Rome as I am. The edict is revoked."

The young man still looked bewildered, and in a few words he was told all that had happened.

"Let me go to her," he said, when it was finished. "You say I am free; I will go to them; I will never leave them again."

"My son," said Tithonius, shortly, "remember we sail to-morrow for Ephesus."

"Father," replied Philip, looking up in his father's face calmly and resolutely, but not disrespectfully, "father I am no longer a child, and I am a Christian. My God has wonderfully preserved my life in the midst of death, and restrained the wrath of his enemies. This he has done because he has yet a work for me to accomplish on earth, and that work does not lie in Ephesus, but in Rome. Had the emperor's edict continued in force, I would have submitted to the law, and left the city ; but now I feel that I must stay here, where I first learned to know my Master I cannot be what you wish me to be; I could not turn my mind to such things now even if I would. There are dying men around me, and I must carry to them the news of life. Let me go."

He went out of the gates, down the street, his father and friend following, but not detaining him, and so he stood once more beside his cousin in the gloomy arches of the Colosseum. He turned aside the rough cloak with which a pitying hand had covered her, and gazed into her face. Her beautiful hair was disordered and soiled with the dust of the blood-stained arena ; with a touch as gentle as a woman's, Philip smoothed it back from her brow. Her hands had fallen at her sides ; he raised them, and crossed them on her breast. There they lay, their work accomplished—

hands that had never moved save in the employment of a loving will. Her lips were slightly apart—the lips from which had so often issued the language of tender sympathy and consolation were silent forever. The eyes were closed; gently the dark-fringed lids lay on the pale cheek. None could evermore look into their depths for love and pity, for the loving, pitying soul no longer looked through windows of flesh. Out of this world, so full of weakness and ignorance, and sorrow and suffering and sin, men had driven the strong, wise, loving angel God had given them.

There was a hand caught Philip by the mantle, and he started from his sad, bewildering dreams. It was the hand of Mutius, the carpenter of the Via Aurea; he had known him in prison. The man held something carefully wrapped in a cloth; it was a set of ivory tablets, a gift from Philip to Marcella long years before.   There were words upon it which quickly drew the young Greek's attention, and he hardly listened to the explanation:

"She gave it to me for you when she knew you had left the prison. I was to have sent it to you, but I could not learn where you were until now."

"Another light!" cried Philip hoarsely. "More light!"

It was Maximus who snatched a torch from a soldier and held it aright, gazing also on the precious words:

"To the hands of the noble Greek, Philip of Ephesus, these, speedily:

"Thou art free. For thee the crown, and the palm, and the rest are not now, but they shall be hereafter. For this I give thanks to our Lord and Saviour that he hath not left his cause without witnesses on the earth. Philip! thou art baptized in blood; be

strong and of good courage. The prison
doors have been opened for thee and closed
upon me, because thy work is not accomplished and mine is. Go on, then, in that
strength which, as thou seest, can overcome
all things, even death. Go not back to the
life. Friends and country, and father and
mother, and sister and brother, must be abandoned if *they* stand on one side and Christ
calleth to the other. Thou hast learning;
use it for thy Master; but remember, though
the head of a Christian may be as the head
of a sage, his heart must be as the heart of a
little child. Forget not that sorrow is often
sent to us that we may have wherewith to
comfort others; and only in thus comforting
others can we ourselves be comforted. Seek
out, if thou canst, Paulina, the daughter of
Paulinus. On the day of our arrest she was
conveyed away by her father; whither I
know not, but doubtless to trials which will

shake her faith to its foundation. She is feeble, and ever needeth a strong and loving heart to keep her aright. Give unto her my greeting, and bid her never lose her grasp on eternal life. Oh, Philip! our enemies think they bestow on us shame, agony, and death, when, instead, they give us rest, peace, eternal life! Thou and I shall meet again ; death cannot divide those who are one in Jesus, one in the hope of a glorious resurrection. Though it seemeth night now, there cometh a morning, and I cannot fear. Farewell until the morning."

"Will there come a morning after such a night ?" said Maximus bitterly ; and Philip looked up in the Roman noble's face to find in it an expression far different from that of the careless happiness which it usually wore ; a look so stern and yet so hopeless, that it awoke his pity even in the midst of his own deep grief, for he knew the depth of that darkness from which he himself had so lately emerged.

"Yes, Maximus ; as surely as the sun will rise to-morrow over Rome, so surely has the light of an eternal day dawned upon the soul which once dwelt in this lifeless form. You think to annihilate life when you only lift it up higher."

"Not I !" exclaimed Maximus, shrinking back; "I had no hand in the infamous deed —the gods be witnesses? But if all this be true, what vengeance will not your God inflict upon us, upon our nation, upon this guilty city?"

Philip might have asked the same question himself a little while before, and it was that thought which made his heart swell with thankfulness as he replied :

"Our God is no God of vengeance, but of infinite, unfathomable love. The most blood-stained hands will grow white when clasped

11*

by the wounded ones of our crucified Brother. Come to him, throw yourself upon his mercy, and he will bestow upon you, even upon you, the gift of eternal life !"

There was a softened look on the Roman's face, an eager, wistful expression in his eyes, but he did not speak ; and at that moment a soldier informed them that, by order of the officer in charge, the bodies must be removed immediately. This order seemed to have been anticipated, for at a sign from Mutius four young men stepped forward with the sun-burnt faces and toil-hardened hands of the fossi, bearing a rude bier. Philip lifted the lifeless body and laid it reverently on cushions formed of the worn garments of the poor men, perhaps their only possession, which they had given so gladly to honor, in their poor way, one who had so long been the sunshine of their homes. Then the bearers stooped to their burden—fit emblem of the heavier burden resting on their saddened hearts. Philip walked at her side, sometimes arranging a fold in the cover, which had become disordered by the motion, but giving no orders. Mutius, with a torch in his hand, led the way.

Maximus and Tithonius walked a little behind, but with different thoughts revolving in their minds. The heart of the old Greek was full of bitter hatred; he had steeled it against sympathy, even against parental affection. No gentle influences came to him from that young martyr's saintly face. He had no tear to shed for his young kinswoman; he only thought of his own baffled plans, the hope of his house taken from him by a far worse blow than would have been an honorable death; and so absorbed was he in his reflections, that he was hardly conscious he was following in the funeral procession.

Maximus also was thinking. His gay, careless heart had been stirred to its very depths.   He had, for the first time in his life, seen and sympathized with real sorrow; and yet, strange to say, it was in connection with it that he first saw real peace and a substantial hope.   He saw death, even in its most painful form, robbed of its terrors, and life invested with a grandeur of purpose which contrasted strongly with his aimless existence. Might not *he* attain this hope?   Could not *he* begin to live for eternity?   At that dead girl's side the pleasures, which had made life to him until now, faded into hollow shows.   His heart was very tender, for the Spirit of God was working powerfully in it.   Almost he was persuaded to be a Christian.   Would he take that one decided step which might bridge over the ever-widening gulf between the "almost" and the "altogether!"   That calm summer evening was the turning-point in his life for time and for eternity, but he did not know it.

The little procession paused at last at one of the entrances to the Catacombs. The torches were retrimmed, and they exchanged the fresh evening air and moonlight for the close, damp smell of the underground passages. They had not far to go. In one of the galleries was an open niche; beside it a slab of stone and mortar. Here the bearers set down their burden.

There were a few men gathered around, Philip could not tell how many; but he heard, as though they came from a great distance, the words of prayer which followed. Very few they were. There is a grief so intense, so absorbing, that even holy words fall on deadened ears. Then they laid her in her narrow bed. So gently, so tenderly they touched her with their clumsy hands, and arranged and re-arranged every fold of her drapery! Then they gathered around and looked at her; gazed for the last time in that

face, so unspeakably precious. And so it
happened that, even as they gazed at her features, their own changed. She who had so
long preached Jesus and the resurrection,
preached the same even from her grave.
That atmosphere of hope, and peace, and
love, which had always surrounded her in
life, clung even around the soulless body,
and radiated from it to those around; for
even as they gazed, the burden seemed
lifted from their hearts. Not that they did
not sorrow, but their sorrow was mingled
with a strange, celestial joy, in which selfish
grief was changed into a cheerful acquies-
cence in God's will; and faith, taking up the
glass of hope, showed to them so plainly
the land beyond the river, that time and
space seemed annihilated, the barriers of
death had vanished, and, in the blessed communion of saints, the Church militant and
triumphant were merged into one, embraced

by one Love, one Lord, one glorious eternal Life!

The last touch of the trowel was given, and the plain slab of stone, shutting up forever from mortal eyes the sacred dust, waited for its inscription. Then Philip spoke:

" Brethren in the Lord! She who sleeps here hath left no kinsman but me to claim a right to weep at her grave, and I—I have been less to her than the least of you. Father and mother are with her in heaven. Write her as the Maiden of Rome; for, for you she lived, with you she died, among you she lies buried."

In the upper air they parted—Tithonius to hasten his departure from a place filled for him with hateful memories, Maximus to toss on his luxurious bed and struggle with the great thoughts crowding into his mind. Philip, his soul steadfastly fixed on the great work before him, silently trod the streets in

the quiet midnight hour at the side of Mutius
the carpenter, and Marcella bore the olive
branch of victory and peace along the golden
streets of heaven.

CHAPTER XII.

Brother and Sister.

EUDORA awoke on the morning of the day appointed for her departure from Rome little pleased with the prospect. Her pretty face, her merry smile, and her gentle, playful ways, had won for her many admirers, and some warm friends. The noble lady Julia, the mother of Maximus, petted and spoiled her; she and his sisters, Sophia and Helena, were bound together by all the confidences, vows and secrets which go to make up girlish friendships, while the flattering attentions of the young noble himself had quite turned her foolish little head, so that her home in Ephesus appeared very lonely by contrast, and the remembrance of her mother's strict rule very distasteful. Nor did her father's manner toward her tend to make the prospect of a long journey with him more inviting. He could not indeed accuse her of any tendency toward Christianity; but his manner was cold and stern; he watched her incessantly, as if he feared that she might bring more disgrace on the already overburdened family; and he would not allow her to have anything to do with Philip, or even to speak of him, and she did love Philip. He had not been the most attentive of brothers to her, he was too indolent and self-indulgent for that, but they had played together as children; they had hardly been separated a day until after their arrival at Rome; he was her brother, and she loved him. And now she would never see him again—her father had told her so—and since that day in the judgment hall when she had seen him bound as a felon, and yet with that strange, glowing light in his eyes, and those still more unaccountable words on his lips, she had never spoken with him; and yet, as she remembered how coldly he had put her aside when she clung pleading to him, how unmoved he had appeared by her grief, she feared that this Christianity, the very name of which was horrible to her, had required him to hate her, and he was trying to do it.

These thoughts absorbed her mind during all the short journey from Rome to the Ostian port, where the ship lay awaiting them; and as she gazed out upon the boundless expanse of blue sea, she only thought how lonely all the great world was, and how much more sorrow and pain there was in it than she had imagined a few short months ago, and wonder if Marcella had done with it all, lying so calmly in her tomb in the Catacombs; and thus it seemed but as an embodiment of her thoughts when, as they stood on the shore exchanging last farewells, Philip joined them. He came up to her directly, took her hand, and turned to his father.

"Are *you* here ?" said Tithonius, speaking first, and moving a step backward.

"Yes," said Philip, "I am here, father; I have come to bid you and my sister a long farewell, and I wish to speak to Eudora alone."

"Speak to Eudora!" exclaimed the Greek, angrily. "Have you not brought us low enough with your folly, that you would drag your sister away to share in your madness and its consequences? Let go her hand; she is no sister of thine, even as I am no father of such a son!"

Philip's cheek grew very pale, and his voice was husky, as he replied :

"My father, I submit to your will; yet let me speak a word with the maiden before we part forever. I will not promise to speak nothing to her of my madness, as you call it, but I will promise neither by word nor deed to seek to withdraw her from you, or to make her other than what a daughter—an only child—should be to a parent."

"Let the girl speak for herself," said Tithonius, turning away; and Philip took both his sister's hands in his and looked down into her face.

"Will you speak with me, Eudora?"

For an answer the girl only flung herself on his neck, weeping passionately. Her brother drew her away to where there were some stone seats sheltered by the high wall of the pier, and seated her by his side. For awhile he let her weep until the tears had expended themselves, and only long, quivering sobs shook her frame. Then she spoke.

"Oh, Philip! why did we ever come to this dreadful place? If we had only never heard of this Christianity we might have been so happy together! You would have been content in Ephesus, and would have become a great philosopher, and our father would have been so proud, but now"—she paused, for the sadness of that *now* overcame her, and she buried her face on his shoulder.

"Well, Eudora, and now?"

"Now it is all sadness and sorrow; I never shall be happy again; how *could* I be without you? We will never see each other again, and they will kill you as they did Marcella."

"Nay, Eudora, I do not think they will do that; there is something within me that tells me a long life is before me, and a great work, and until that is accomplished nothing can harm me."

"But oh, Philip, the honor! You have often said that life was worth nothing without glory. Don't you remember in the garden at home, where we played, that you were the young Sophocles, contending for the prize with Ædipus, and I crowned you with laurel leaves, and you threw them down and trampled on them, saying it was nothing, because the whole world was not there to see?"

Philip smiled at the remembrance of the boundless ambition of his childhood, when the world seemed too small to limit his future exploits, and language too poor to sound his praise.

"Yes, Eudora, I remember it well; but strange as it may seem to you, I see before me a height of glory far surpassing that which dazzled my childish vision, a contest the prize for which is as far above all earthly treasures as a golden, jewelled crown is above our fillet of laurel leaves; and that height of glory I believe I shall attain; that contest I have entered upon, that crown I believe I shall gain. Dear Eudora, as I look out upon the sea that brought us hither, I love it. I bless those walls within which I first found out what life truly is. Now I truly live, for I know that I shall live forever. When the ship in which we came dropped anchor by these very steps a few short months ago, I little thought of the blessing which awaited me where I only thought to find pleasure. I thank God for my *now*, for in it is comprehended a hereafter so glorious, so blissful, that my very soul melts in rapture at the thought."

"I cannot understand you," said Eudora sadly; "I cannot see anything but gloom and misery. But what will you do—how can you live here all alone?"

"I do not know," said her brother. "I have heard that once, when a servant of God was hungry, he sent ravens to feed him, morning and evening, and I know that not even a sparrow falls to the ground without my Father's knowledge, and he cannot let his children want."

"But, Philip," said Eudora, not comprehending, "our father is so very angry, he says he will not leave you a drachma. Oh, Philip! —it was so horrible—he said if you came to him begging he would not give you a piece of bread."

The color flushed into the young Greek's face, and the tears filled his eyes; but he answered without bitterness, though very sadly:

"I meant my Father in heaven, Eudora. He has promised that he will never leave nor forsake me, and I believe he will give me strength to earn my daily bread while I do his work. Oh, Eudora, if you only knew! if you could only understand! How can I let you go without the blessing of gospel peace! It is you who are going out into a cold world without a guide, not I ; it is you who are to tread the rough ways of life without a heavenly Father's watchful care, a divine Brother's loving sympathy ; it is you that the angels pity. Oh, my little sister that I love so dearly—I never knew how dearly till now—I could gladly see you forsaken by all the world, aye, I could see you stand, as Marcella stood, in the bloody Colosseum, if I only knew that you had laid hold on eternal life, if you had only given yourself into the hands of a crucified Redeemer ; and that you may yet be led to do so, even though far away from me, I will pray to my God with all my heart and soul and strength, until he grant my request and I meet you in heaven."

" Philip, don't talk so !" cried Eudora, drawing herself away from his passionate embrace. " You frighten me so ! Do not pray to your God for me—do not let him have anything to do with me. I only want the old times. I do not want to believe in him; he cannot be anything but cruel when he takes you away from me, and makes you want me to be murdered like Marcella. See! they are wanting me, the boat is waiting, I must go."

It was even so; their short interview was over, and Philip could not see that that gay, trifling spirit had been touched by anything but the momentary pain of parting from him. He did not attempt to say anything more, but left her with a slight pressure of the hand as he saw his father approaching, and turned away until he found a spot on the porch of one of the buildings, where, secure from observation, he leaned against a pillar, and watched the vessel depart. He saw the rowers taking their seats; saw the long oars drop, splashing, into the water; saw Eudora waving gaily to Maximus and other friends who stood upon the pier; watched, as in a dream, the vessel slowly receding, line after line being gradually blotted out and blending into a dusky speck, until at last even that disappeared, and nothing was left but the blue sea, the cloudless sky, and a weary, aching heart. Then he turned toward the city.

Maximus had just passed in his luxurious chariot, but *he* had no such conveyance ; and the inconvenience of the dust and heat reminded him that the last piece of money obtained by selling his superfluous articles of wearing apparel and jewelry lay in his purse, and he knew not where to turn to gain any more. He could not bear to be any longer dependent on the poor people who had until now sheltered him, although they never seemed to grudge him his humble bed or his share of their simple repasts ; but he had hands that could learn to labor, even though they were now soft and feeble, and the sooner they began the better.

With these thoughts in his mind he sought the workshop of his friend Mutius, and stood by him watching, while the white chips flew from under his tool, and the wood assumed fair proportions under his dextrous hands.

"Mutius," said Philip, "it does not seem so hard to do that; let me try it."

Mutius put the tool in his hand, and showing him how to use it, left him with a block of wood to try upon, and the young Greek fell manfully to work. His blows fell fast and thick, but the iron seemed to slip from the wood without leaving any impression upon it; he had already wounded himself more than once, his whole body ached, and the sweat stood in great drops on his forehead. At last he dropped the mallet, and leaned panting against the work-bench.

"Mutius, I cannot do it. I have neither skill nor strength; how shall I earn my bread?"

"Do not be troubled, sir," said the carpenter kindly; "you are not used to this; you will be stronger by and by; and, beside, there is other work in the world beside handwork. You are welcome to anything I have; but if you would rather, I will seek for something that will suit you better."

So a few days after, Mutius came to Philip, and with many apologies for the humbleness of the occupation, told him that he had found an old basket-maker who needed an assistant and would teach him his trade.

"My Master was a carpenter, and his apostles tent-makers and fishermen," said Philip. "I am glad to be like them even in this;" and the young Greek philosopher sat down at the old basket-maker's feet, and bent all his energies to his novel employment. It was not easy work. The stubborn twigs seemed determined to resist all attempts to bend them without breaking them, and baskets, rough and misshapen, fell to pieces in the endeavor to make them stand upright; but he labored on patiently, if not unweariedly, and at last was rewarded by success; and as he carried his first firm, well-made basket home to the person who had ordered it, he felt for the first time the pleasures which ensue even from Adam's curse.

So he passed a quiet, uneventful life, the consciousness gradually growing upon him that this was just the discipline that was best for him. He was improving in health, strength, and dexterity; nor was basket-making the only thing he learned from his master, for Decius was a humble but well-instructed Christian, and many were the pleasant and profitable conversations that filled their minds with sweet and comforting thoughts, while their fingers were occupied with their daily toil. The highly-educated young Greek could throw light upon some points which had

seemed dark to the basket-maker, while the
old man could draw from the experience of a
long life of faith and obedience many useful
lessons; and they sat side by side each Sabbath in the little chapel to hear the story
which can never be heard too often, and learn
the lessons which life is too short to comprehend, and eternity alone can fully develop.

CHAPTER XIII.

Marcella's Legacy.

ALL this time Philip had not forgotten the legacy left him by Marcella—the care of the Lady Paulina, and had endeavored many times to discover what had become of her, but in vain. The palace in the Via Sacra was closed, and Pollonius was reported to be staying at one of his villas near Capua; but Philip, after many dangerous, as well as wearisome investigations, discovered that his daughter did not form part of his household; and Cyril, the only one of his slaves to whom he dared confide the reason of his inquiries, gave him little encouragement. There were other ways, he said, of disposing of Christians

12*

beside the public condemnation in the judgment-hall.   It was evident that the Roman
noble dreaded above all things lest the world
should know that one of his own flesh and
blood belonged to the sect he so hated and
despised, and, to the father who had not hesitated to drive that shrinking weeping girl
from his threshold out into the stormy night,
it might not have been difficult to descend to
even more fearful crimes; and the slave's
voice lowered as he told how his master's
drunken revels were continuing night after
night; how even those few companions de-
praved enough to join him in his feastings as
in his feuds were dropping off one by one;
how he grew, day by day, more fiercely tyran-
nical toward his slaves, and yet so fearful and
suspicious that he would not stir from his
gates unless accompanied by an armed guard;
and how it was darkly whispered among his
dependents that either the blood of the

Roman maiden and her companion, in the Colosseum was crying to the gods for vengeance, or else it was another crime, too hideous to have a name, which was filling his waking hours with horrid fears, and his sleeping ones with still more horrid dreams.

Philip turned away sad and hopeless; sad, more for the miserable father than for the helpless child, for he believed that that timid gentle spirit was already walking with Marcella the streets of the City of Peace; and from that time he gave up the search, and went on quietly with his daily labor, until the short winter had passed, and the Campagna was beautiful with spring flowers; then one afternoon he took a boat and went up the river to receive some bundles of osiers which he needed for his work. It was a perfect day, and there was no need of haste, so, on returning, he drew in his oars, and suffered the boat to float down with the tide, while he drank in the loveliness of the scene, and wondered what must be the glories of that heaven which lay in store for him, if its beauties far exceeded all that ear ever heard, or eye beheld, or imagination conceived. He was roused from his revery by a little cry of wonder and delight—

" Oh ! Philip, Philip ! is it you ?"

He started and seized his oars, looking on all sides for the voice, but at first he could not see whence it had proceeded. His boat had floated, drawn by an eddy, so close to the shore, that it was entangled by the reeds, and it needed all his exertions, for a moment, to prevent it from grounding in the mud ; but, as by a vigorous push he shoved it off, he saw that just above him was a little summer-house, or covered seat, projecting from a wall that evidently surrounded a villa of some extent, though of dilapidated appearance, and from it looked down upon him a pale, eager face, that he had never expeected to see in this world again. It took him but a few moments to land, a friendly tree and some vines aided his ascent, and in a few moments more he was standing by the Lady Paulina's side.

She could not speak to him for some moments, but only sobbed out her gladness that some one had found her at last, while Philip could only look at her, and wonder at the change that sorrow and suspense had wrought in the sweet, childish face, that he had last seen nestling in Marcella's bosom. All the sweetness was there still, but there was such a look of settled suffering in the dimmed, brown eyes, the pallid cheeks, and the quivering lips, that he trembled at the thought of what those months of agony must have been.

"Tell me all about Marcella," she said, at last; "don't be afraid to tell me all; I know that she is dead."

The young Greek told all about those fearful days, and wondered that the delicate girl at his side did not seem to shrink from their horrors; he did not know that life had become so bitter to her, that even a death among the lions in the Colosseum seemed preferable to it. Then she told her tale.

On the day when the Christians were surprised at their worship in the underground chapel, she had felt herself seized by two men, wrapped in a cloak, and borne rapidly away in another direction from that taken by the rest of the captives. She heard her father's voice giving some directions, in which she could only distinguish the "Tiber," and she believed she was to be thrown into the river. She lost consciousness then, and only recovered it to find herself in a strange room, barely furnished, and having only a window, high up in the wall, opening into an inner court. This room, and another opening from it, she had never left until a few days before, and all that time she had been waited on by an old woman and a rough-looking man whom she had never before seen, and who turned a deaf ear to her pleadings for news of her friends. She had seen her father twice, and he had assured her that every Christian in Rome was slain. After each of these visits she believed there had been an attempt made to murder her, but some little circumstance, ordered by a watchful Providence, had interfered to thwart their plans. Once she had been very ill, she believed from the effect of something they had mixed with her food, she did not know how long, but after that the old woman had been a little kinder to her, and now allowed her to wander in the deserted garden a part of every day. The strain upon her nerves while thus daily expecting a violent death must have been dreadful, especially when added to the depressing effects of loneliness ; nothing but Christian principle could have borne up against it.

"I told it all to Jesus," she said, "when I was so lonely, and thought every one that loved me was dead, and only those that hated me were alive; and when I was so thirsty and did not dare to drink, and he used to come and comfort me. Sometimes I thought I saw him moving in the room, and then it was all light, and he would say, 'Peace be unto you.' Then I would fall asleep and dream of Marcella walking among the angels; and when I called her she would come out from their company, and put her cool hand on my brow, and kiss me, just as she used to do ; but when I asked her to let me come there too among the happy angels, she would always say, 'Not yet, not yet!' so I knew I was not to die yet, and Christ would give me strength not to be so frightened. Sometimes, when I remembered my father's words, I thought that perhaps God did not care any more for Rome now there were no Christians in it; but at other times it seemed as if perhaps Jesus might love me all the more, and watch me all the closer, if there were no others to guard from danger and save in temptation. Only it seemed as if death would be so sweet if there were only some one to hold my hand when I was going. This evening it seemed as if those crimson and golden glories were only curtains that hid Marcella from me, and I stretched out my hand toward them; and then, through a little rift in the clouds, just where the evening star always came first, she seemed to look down on me with her beautiful eyes full of love and joy and hope, and pointed down to the earth, and then I saw you."

"She sent me to you," said Philip, with tears in his eyes; "she bade me seek you, and give you her greeting, and charged me to watch over you, and give you a helping hand, that you might never lose your hold on the eternal life she is enjoying."

"Did she?" said the girl, laying both her hands in those Philip held out to her, and lifting her face in childlike simplicity and confidence. "Oh, I am so thankful! I am so weak; so very, very weak. I was so afraid that I might yield in some moment when they pressed me so hard; but now, if you will only comfort me a little, and tell me things to strengthen me, and if I can only think you are praying for me that my faith fail not when the doubt and fear come, then I shall be able to stand firm; but oh, it was so horrible to feel so all alone!"

"It must have been very horrible," said Philip, gathering the two little hands in one of his, and putting the disengaged arm around the trembling waist.

"I suppose I ought not to have felt so.

Marcella used to say that Jesus would never forsake me, and I know now he never does. I suppose it was weakness in me, but I did so want to talk to some one who was just like myself, and would tell me what other people were doing; and now you have come! But you are so wise—Marcella said you were—and you will think I am a very weak, foolish child, but please be kind to me, there is no one left to love me now; but please help me a little for her sake!"

Philip gazed down into the sweet face raised so pitifully toward his, and his heart was swelling with so many thoughts that none could shape themselves into words; only he felt that the charge Marcella had laid upon him would be no heavy burden to bear through life.

As the little boat shot down the river in the starlight, impelled by far more vigorous strokes than those which it had felt in ascending the stream, Philip felt his heart strangely lightened. Life seemed opening to him, hope and fancy revived. There was one in the world for whose happiness he might live, for whom he might labor with heart and hand. Already he was laying a thousand plans.

The next day he informed the basket-maker and Mutius of the situation in which he had found the persecuted young Christian. They knew the situation of the villa in question, and that its remoteness and apparent abandonment rendered it peculiarly fitted for the scene of any dark deed; and all agreed that the young girl ought to escape from it as soon as possible, for if Pollonius suspected her of any communication with the Christians, her fate would be instantly sealed; and even if Philip's visit was undiscovered, there was no telling when her father might send her away to some other place of concealment, where they might be unable to reach her at all. But many difficulties presented them-selves. Her father would soon discover her flight, and all Rome would be scoured to find her. She must be closely concealed until the search was over, or else hurried away to some foreign country, which must thenceforth be her home, and who was there that could do this? It was true that the Catacombs were always ready as a place of refuge, and there were many among the poor fossi who would gladly provision the retreat from their own scanty stores, but who was there to take charge of her in her secret journey, and where was she to find a home in a foreign land?

They took all their troubles to the minister who presided over the chapel they attended, and, with him, they found the bishop who had been chosen in the place of the one that had sealed his faith with his blood in the Colos-seum with Marcella. They both thought that a retreat should be immediately provided for her, and that there she should remain, under the protection of the bishop's sister, until they could lay other plans. God would open them a way.

Philip waited, at the bishop's desire, till his companions had departed, and then told him the hopes that had filled his own mind.

"I am only a basket-maker," he said, "but I can earn my own bread, and hers too ; and Marcella put her in my charge. We are both fatherless, motherless, homeless. If you will give her to me for a wife, I believe our heavenly Father will bless us with his favor, and we shall not want."

"Are these truly your thoughts, my son?" said the bishop, seriously. "Remember, marriage is not a matter of convenience or pity, or even of kindness. Unless love accompany it as well as duty, it is only a bitter mockery, a dangerous snare."

Philip thought of the sweet eyes that looked so trustingly into his; of the gentle voice that had called to him with such eager joy across the river, and he was not afraid.

"And now," continued the bishop, "I, too, have a plan, and one which now seems to be most providentially arranged to aid us at this juncture. Philip of Ephesus! the Lord hath other work for thee beside basket-making. He has not given thee a cultivated mind, a keen intellect, an earnest heart, and a ready tongue for naught. Wilt thou use them for his service?"

Philip looked up, surprised.

"I hardly know what you mean; the schools in which I have *learned* are not those where *God's* knowledge is taught."

"You have been in the schools of affliction and humiliation," said the bishop, emphatically, "and in them you have learned a philosophy such as Socrates and Plato could not instil, and an endurance such as was not learned in Sparta. The Church has watched you these months, and now claims you. In Helvetia, among the snowy Alps, a little band of Christians has assembled, driven by persecution from their former homes, and many of the natives have learned of them the truth that makes free. They have sent to me for a pastor to lead them in their devotions, and to carry the gospel light to many that sit in darkness. When that call came, and I looked around upon those who had passed through this last fiery trial, and so have learned, by deep experience, the preciousness of a crucified Redeemer, I thought of you."

"Let me think," said Philip rising and drawing his cloak around him; for he felt as if he must be alone in the pure fresh air with this mighty thought so suddenly thrust upon him. The good bishop understood his feelings too well to seek to detain him; he only laid his hand on his shoulder, and said very solemnly:

"Yes, my son, consider and decide, and in all your considerations mingle prayer for the aid of the Spirit of Wisdom. Neither shrink in selfish dread from the responsibilities to which thou art so plainly called by God's providence, nor rush into them unaware of their magnitude, and unprepared for their burden. Ask counsel only of God, and thine own soul; no man can aid thee in this matter. Farewell."

Philip rushed out into the darkness, bending his steps without knowing why, toward the Via Sacra, and down that street, until the huge walls of the Colosseum threw a dark shadow over his way. There he paused a moment irresolutely, then entered. The building was deserted, and by the cold light of the waning moon, which gleamed in at the windows, casting fantastic shadows on the

13

stone pavements of the galleries and stair-
ways, and flooding with light the smooth
expanse of white sand in the arena, he
mounted to the very highest tier, and threw
himself upon a bench.

Here he felt himself alone; yes, fearfully
alone. Of all the thousands who had so
lately thronged the place, nobles and plebeians, actors and spectators, not one was left;
the loneliness was almost oppressive. But
the Tempter was there, and in that stillness
and desolation wrestled with the young Greek
for his soul.

For, as he sat there on the stone seat, his
face buried in his hands, the ambition of his
childhood, which he had long thought dead
and buried beneath the waters of baptism,
arose and confronted him in a form so
enticing, so subtile, and so attractive, that he
yielded to its attractions and revelled in its
delights.   He knew that he possessed the

gift of eloquence, and here was an opportunity of bringing all his powers to bear on a
theme worthy of his utmost efforts. He saw
men moved by his burning words, rushing in
crowds to receive at his hands the waters of
baptism, and tearing down their heathen
temples to elevate in their stead more majestic ones to the Christian's God. He saw
aristocratic disgust conquered, and even royal
rage subdued by the magic of his lips ; and
Christianity raised from the religion of the
fossi to the doctrine of the palace ; and all
this was to be accomplished, not by the Spirit
of Jesus of Nazareth, but by the intellect of
Philip of Ephesus !

But as his dreams were mounting even
higher, a sound brought him to his feet. It
was not the wind moaning among the arches,
although he thought it was at first. A second
time he heard it, and then he knew what it
was—the roar of the lions in their dungeons

beneath him. He started, passed his hands over his eyes, and gazed down upon the shining sand. He seemed to see, as it had so often been described to him, that little group issuing from the gloomy arch, to hear the faint, sweet notes of the chanted psalm, to see the rush and bound of the savage beasts, and to tremble at the agonizing cries of the victims.

In a moment he saw his own thoughts in the light of that bloody scene, and with a cry of horror, he leaped over the low parapet, rushed along the passages and staircases, and never paused until he reached the arched chamber where he had last seen Marcella; and by the stone bench on which she had been laid in her blood-stained raiment, he flung himself on his knees and wept.

CHAPTER XIV.

The Price of Blood.

THE following evening saw the little boat again ascending the Tiber, but this time with two occupants, for Philip felt that he should not encounter single-handed the difficulties which he might have to overcome in placing the Lady Paulina in the retreat prepared for her in the Catacombs, and he trusted much to the ready wit of Mutius, and his knowledge of the ground, as well as to his strong arm.

Their ostensible errand was to procure reeds, and they did, indeed, so load their boat with them that it appeared like a floating bower, and when it was drawn up among the tall grass beneath the summer-house, no one at a little distance would have been able to distinguish it from the waving, swaying green by which it was surrounded. Mutius was left in charge of it while Philip climbed the bank, for he had yet to persuade the timid girl to trust herself in their hands, and expose herself to those dangers which would be the consequence of attempting to escape from the power of one at once so powerful and malignant.

She was tremblingly glad to see Philip, and he thought he could already perceive the change for the better which returning hope and an assurance of sympathy had made on the wan face. She said that she had been undisturbed since he had been there before, but that the old woman had looked suspiciously at her, and that the man who had charge of her had gruffly remonstrated against the permission given her to walk in the garden, and she was afraid she was watched, or that perhaps they were going to take her away to some other place, and if they did, what should she do? She had thought she could bear it all, now that she knew there was some one to come for her, yet this made it seem harder than ever not to see him again. That evening when she had first come to the summer-house, and looked up and down the river without seeing him, she had thought that perhaps the interview of the night before was only a bright, happy dream, such as had often tantalized her in her feverish nights, but which was only a dream after all.

"It was true," said Philip, gently, "and I have come to prove it to you. Lady Paulina, will you trust me?"

The girl looked up wonderingly into his eyes, but she seemed to be satisfied with what she saw there, for she laid her hand in his arm, and said, simply: "Marcella said so, and I will. I will do what you think best."

"Then," said Philip, "I will tell you frankly that I think you are in great danger here, and that we, your friends, think you must immediately leave this place and go to one that has been prepared for you, where you will at least be safe for a time."

She started. To her timid spirit, and nerves unstrung by mental and bodily suffering, every change seemed fraught with fear; but, before she could speak, they both turned pale with alarm. There were heavy footfalls on the garden path, and a rough voice, which the poor girl knew only too well, and she clung, gasping, to her companion for protection. Not a moment was to be lost. He made a low call, such as the wild birds often make in winging their way over the Campagna, and, in a moment, Mutius' head appeared above the bushes, as he balanced himself in the boat. Meanwhile the footsteps were drawing nearer, and Philip saw that Paulina was, with difficulty, repressing a scream, so he put his hand upon her lips, and whispered: "Be very quiet; you said you would trust me; do not make a sound, whatever happens;" and then, gathering her in one arm, he swung himself down the bank—how, he could never tell—and clung with one hand to a tree, until he felt her safe in the grasp of Mutius. The latter who had turned over the reeds and laid the almost unconscious girl in the bottom of the boat, piled them again over, and scarcely had Philip sprung to his place, before a vigorous push of the oars sent the boat out into the middle of the stream. Nor were they a moment too soon, for already two dark forms appeared in the little summer-house, and a curse and shout rang out over the water:

13*

" What boat is that ? "

The two young men bent all their energies to their task, and the oars bent under
their sturdy strokes. But the boat was
small and overburdened, and, ere they had
passed a mile on their way, they felt sure
they were pursued.   In the perfect stillness
of the night they could hear the measured
beat of oars in the water, and once, just as
they were rounding a bend in the river, they
perceived the waving of torches scarcely half
a mile behind them. Philip gave up all for
lost, and would have thrown down his oars in
despair, had not Mutius whispered to him
that there was one more chance to be tried,
and, turning the boat toward the left bank,
at the same moment tossing overboard the
whole cargo of reeds, he left them to float
down the river on the rapid tide. The boat,
meanwhile, had entered a broad ditch or
meadow-drain, whose mouth was so overhung

with bushes and vines that it would hardly be noticed in the day-time—much less would it be likely to attract attention at night. The moon, too, was past its full, and only just rising. The ditch ran for some distance in a direction parallel with the river, so that in a little while they were side by side with their pursuers, only a fringe of low bushes between. They rested on their oars, and hardly dared to breathe, as the glare of the torches flashed through the leafy screen, and hoarse voices were heard calling to each other.

Philip felt Paulina's trembling clasp upon him, and heard her quick, sobbing breath; but, in trustful obedience, she had not uttered a word. When the boat had passed, he raised her from her cramped position, and said, in a tremulous voice:

"Thank God! we are safe now!"

"Hardly," whispered Mutius: "they will soon overtake the floating reeds, and finding what they are will return to seek us; we must be away from here as soon as possible. There is no use in attempting to enter the city, for they will, no doubt, have warned the guards at all the river gates."

"But the retreat," said Philip; "that is within the walls."

"There are other ways of entering the Catacombs besides those you have seen," was the reply. "There used to be one near here, and, if it is still practicable, we will soon reach it. We will land here."

They did so, plunging for some distance through the mud and wet grass, Philip carrying Paulina, while Mutius, after giving the little boat a push that sent it floating slowly down the ditch, lest it might betray the secret of their landing-place, went in front to pick out the firmest spots for them to tread upon. They soon reached higher ground. The moon shone out brightly, and the night breeze, which had sprung up, was very re-freshing to their fevered frames.

When the entrance was found, it proved to be a sort of pit, formed by the caving in of the earth, at a point where the excavation had approached too near the surface, De-scending its side they found a hole partly concealed by weeds, and barely large enough to admit them one at a time, creeping on hands and knees. But once within, Mutius lighted a torch, and they found themselves in the familiar galleries. Philip's heart beat freely again, and he felt his strength renewed; but they had still a long way to go in the narrow, winding passages, sometimes mount-ing, sometimes descending stairs, sometimes clambering over piles of rubbish, and fre-quenty obliged to stop and rest on account of their more feeble companion; but at last they came into the more frequented part of the vast labyrinth; lights gleamed, the space became more open, friendly voices were heard, and the weary girl felt motherly arms around her, and, sinking her head on the kind shoulder, she wept for very joy.

"Let her be with me a little while," said the bishop's sister, the Lady Helena, as she saw the startled look in the timid eyes, when they met the curious glances of those standing around, "She can hardly realize yet that she is safe among friends."

They all left her to the repose she so much needed, and though the chamber was small and stony, it was filled with such an atmosphere of tender love and protecting care as the poor forsaken child had hardly ever dreamed of, and its influence was so sweet to her that she soon forgot all her dangers in a peaceful slumber.

The next morning the Christians were greatly surprised to find that there seemed to be no search made for the Lady Paulina.

At first they suspected that this was only a trap meant to catch them the more completely when they were off their guard; but as day after day passed without any new developments, they could only wonder and be thankful. They believed that the cruel father, only wishing to rid himself of what he conceived to be a burden and disgrace, was too glad to have his daughter off his hands to trouble himself to seek her. But such was not exactly the case.

On the morning after their escape, he was pacing the atrium of his palace, when a slave announced that two men desired to see him. He turned pale, but ordered to be them at once conducted to his presence, and there entered two rough, brutal-looking men, with slouching gait and muffled faces. Sergius Pollonius waved his slaves away, and then the three men stood and looked at each other. Of all the countless faces in the world, there

could hardly have been picked out three so
hateful and so hating; so distorted by every
fierce passion which finds a resting-place in
the human breast — so unmitigatedly *bad.*
They stood for a moment looking at each
other, then Pollonius spoke:

"I suppose, from your coming here, that
you have done your work, and want your
pay."

One of the men muttered something like
assent, but the other, giving his companion a
sly push, at the same moment, with his elbow,
said:

"She will not trouble you again; but if you
would like to see the body——"

"It is not necessary," replied the Roman
noble, his face turning a dull gray ash-color at
the words. The men looked at each other
with a sneer. "You shall have your gold," he
said, and turned away to fetch it, but stag-
gered, and caught at the door-post.

"Coward!" muttered the elder ruffian.

"Just as well he should be so," replied the other, with a peculiarly horrid laugh; "if he were as brave as thou art, we might not have our gold, or our lives either. It would not be so easy to bring him proof if he demanded it, though, to be sure, there are a plenty of young girls' bodies to be had for the seeking, and he would not be the one to look close enough to find out the difference."

"But suppose she were to come back herself some time?" said the elder.

"No danger," was the reply; "she would be a fool, indeed, to come back, when she had once got off so cleverly among friends."

"All women are fools," growled the elder.

"Sayest thou so, friend Pauthus? then it were a pity we have lost the opportunity of ridding the world of one more of them; but, for my part, I am well content; purse full and hands clean is better luck than usual. By the gods! thou and I are none too good; but if I were like that man that thinks himself as fine as the emperor, I would hang myself for very shame at being my own mother's son."

"Cease thy prating," said Pauthus; "here he comes."

Sergius Pollonius entered with the same ashen pallor on his face, and a dull, staring look in his eyes, and handed to each his portion in silence. The elder ruffian received his share in the same way, and only waiting to secure it under his robe, turned toward the door, but the other tossed his up once or twice, as though trying its weight, then laid his hand familiarly on the Roman's arm.

"Hark ye! friend, we have done this business nicely for you; don't forget us now you are rid of all your troubles. We are always ready to serve you if you should want anything else; if, for instance, your house should be lonely, and you should want another daughter."

His hand was flung off as if it had been a viper, and the Roman, crimson with rage, would have felled him to the ground but that the arm stretched out for the purpose trembled too much to perform its office, and, with his low, mocking laugh, the man was gone before he could summon assistance.

At the same moment the curtains which concealed a door leading into an inner apartment were drawn back, and a young girl stepped out before him.

"You have given these men gold; give me some, also; I deserve it as well!"

"Who are you?" exclaimed Pollonius, gazing angry and amazed at the strange figure before him. The past year had not improved the appearance of the child who had scorned Marcella's love, and betrayed her into the hands of her enemies. Wild and unkempt she had always been, but now her cheeks were pale and her eyes hollow with hunger, and her clothing, soiled and tattered, seemed to add to her deformity rather than conceal it ; nevertheless, she had lost none of her pride and fearlessness, as might be seen by the flash of her eyes and the confidence of her manner. She seemed almost too angry at his non-recognition of her to speak.

"No! no doubt you do not know me. I gave you your revenge, and you promised me that there should be no Christians left, and see how you have kept your promise! The Christians walk the streets of Rome with their heads as high as you do, and I am dying with hunger. Yes, dying with hunger, while they eat and drink their fill, and curse your gods and mine!"

"Who are you, I say?" thundered the Roman. "Am I to be always insulted in my own halls? What are your gods or your hunger to me? Ho! Cyril! Zetus! turn this beggar's brat from the door!"

The child's whole frame dilated with passion, her eyes flashed, her swarthy cheeks burned, while a white line settled around her mouth, and every limb quivered.

"Hold, Gentile dog! I am the child of no beggar, but the daughter of Melchior, priest of Jehovah in the temple of Jerusalem, and I hate and despise you-and your nation, who have laid that temple and city in ashes, only less than I· hate and despise and spit upon the Christians whose crucified prophet profaned it with his presence!"

The Roman smiled grimly, and beckoned again to his slaves, but they stood terrified at the creature, who, seeing that the revelation of her parentage produced only scorn, actually foamed with rage.

"Yes, yes!" she screamed, "scorn me and

my God as you will, he has conquered your gods before, and he will again. Curses upon you ! Do you think others keep their promises to you any more than you have kept yours to me? I could tell you somewhat of those men and of your daughter that you do not know, but I will not ; no, not if you kneeled to me, and offered me all the gold in your palace ! Curses on you !"

Pollonius made one bound toward her, and, with an oath, seized her by the arm ; but she wrenched herself loose, and leaving in his grasp only a handful of her rags, fled with a mocking laugh, out into the street, and was lost in a moment in the passing throng.

And Pollonius was left to the torment of his own memory. Drown it as he might in the wine-cup and the bacchanalian song, thoughts would intrude themselves, and could not be banished ; and ever through those deserted rooms he saw a form gliding before

him ; and sleeping or waking, alone or in
company, the cry was ever in his ears:

"Not alone in the storm, father! Not out
into the night!"

CHAPTER XV.

Gathered Threads.

THE days that followed were peaceful and happy ones to the young Christian girl in her gloomy retreat. She spent her time partly in learning from her kind protectress those little feminine arts of which her position had left her ignorant, and she felt as proud of a well-mended rent in a robe, or a savory dish prepared by her hands, as Philip had of his first firm, upright basket.

She had improved very much in character since the time when Marcella had trembled at the very thought of suffering for her. The suffering had come, far more severe in its lengthened agony than the short, sharp pang of death her friend had anticipated for her, but, sanctified by a submissive heart, directed by a wise and loving will, it had ennobled instead of crushing her. Three months of desertion and loneliness had given her a self-reliance which all the wise counsels of Marcella had not been able to instill, and the absence of all human companionship had given her opportunities for communion with God, and for musing on the highest themes, which could not have been without their influence in elevating and strengthening her mind. She was still weak and timid, but her affections, so rudely torn from their natural support, began to cling closer, day by day, around those dear friends in whose warm, tender affections she felt so protected, so at rest.

Philip saw her every evening when his day's work was completed, and often, after the first fear was over, took her for a walk in

the quiet streets when the stars were shining,
and the evening breeze sweeping cool and
fresh over the heated city ; and she learned
to look forward to these walks as the greatest
pleasure of her quiet life. It was strange to
see how they seemed to become necessary to
each other, although their characters appeared
at first sight so different. She gloried in his
strength and wisdom, as he honored her fee-
bleness and simplicity; he found himself im-
parting to her his highest aspirations and
most profound thoughts, and though she
never attempted either to soar to his heights,
or fathom his depths, or untangle his mysteries, proved the best of listeners ; and with
woman's tact, and the acuteness of love, threw
over her ignorance such a veil of sympathy,
that he imagined there was no one in the
world who understood him so well. Then, it
was as pleasant for him to receive those little
female attentions of which he had been so

long deprived, as it was to her to bestow, what it is every true woman's delight to bestow on one so appreciative, and it was hard to tell which face expressed most delight— his, sunburnt with labor, but glowing with quiet joy as he stooped his tall head to enter the little, cell-like apartment, or hers, flushed with expectation, with eyes beaming, and voice trembling with eagerness.

So it did not seem strange to her when, during one of these walks, he told her of his life-work, and asked her if she should be afraid to go with him to his distant home, that thus they might ever walk side by side the road of life, and so, passing through the gate at its end, walk, still side by side, the streets of the Eternal City; she only said, very simply:

"I will go wherever you go, Philip."

When the autumn came, and the fields of ripened grain on the Campagna surged like a golden sea, they were married, and went away to their distant home. The Christians never indulged in the rough merriment of their heathen neighbors on such occasions, but sanctified the tender tie by prayer, and the reception of the Holy Communion. The evening before their departure, he and his young wife spent a long hour at the tomb of Marcella. Philip had spent many hours there, especially just before and after his ordination, and Paulina too had frequently visited it, for it was a common thing for those who had known and loved her to pause at her place of rest as they passed to and from the chapel, and talk in whispers of her loving deeds and gentle words, and strive to keep alive in their children's minds the memory of her whose blessing had rested upon their infancy; but this was a solemn visit for them both, for they felt that they were bidding farewell to what was more precious to them than anything beside in the imperial city. What passed there they only knew, but Paulina came back with a depth of expression on her face that its childish features had never known before, and Philip with that strange brilliancy in his eyes that had been there when, in the judgment-hall, he had openly professed his faith and submitted himself to those bonds which were to him the type of the only true liberty.

In one of the loveliest of the Helvetian valleys they found their home. Above their heads rose the giant snow-capped mountains, with glittering glaciers and thundering avalanches; before them lay the blue transparent waters of a lake; around them were gathered the cottages of the little hamlet, clustered about their simple, rustic church. The pastor's cottage, hardly to be distinguished from the rest, stood but a stone's throw from the church, with its tiny vineyard terraced against the cliff, and its bit of green lawn lapped at its lower border by the waters of the lake.

There, at its door, sat the pastor one evening with his noble figure and intellectual face. He had not forgotten his old trade of basket-making, for even then he was forming a circle of reeds, stuck upright in the sand, and weaving between them his willow twigs. He only looked up to greet, with his peculiarly happy smile, his wife, who was descending the rocks from the pasture with a pail of milk on her head, and leading a white kid by a string. But she did not answer his greeting at once; she stopped to speak to an old man, who, blind and feeble, had arrested her steps. She spoke to him in her usual gentle, kindly tone, and lowered her pail to give him the drink he requested, but as he was thanking her, a strange change came over her features, the color fled from her face, and she sprang shrieking into the arms of her husband, who had advanced to meet her. She could not speak the cause of her agitation, but Philip, glancing at the beggar's face, altered as it was by disease and misery, comprehended it all. He spoke a few soothing words to her, then went to the blind man and took his hand in his.

" Sergius Pollonius, welcome to our home. Thou art wearied with the dust and heat of the way, let us refresh thee ;—thy daughter and me."

Pollonius did not resist, but when he was seated in the porch, and a cup of milk handed to him, he could not drink, but pushed it away.

" My daughter ;—my child ! I killed her !" Paulina left her husband's arm, where she had been clinging all the while, and went to her father.

" No, father ; God saved me. I am here to comfort and love you."

He put out his arm and drew her to him, holding her fast while he passed the other hand over her hair and features, Those blind, feeble motions touched her deeply, she flung her arms around his neck, his head rested on her bosom, and tears poured from the sightless eyes. Philip turned away and left the father and daughter together.

After awhile they learned his story.

When remorse for his child's murder had made him plunge into even deeper depths of dissipation and crime, the emperor's attention was attracted to his enormities. Some unguarded word, spoken at a drunken revel, had been represented as a treasonable plot, and the many enemies he had made by his tyranny and cruelty in the days of his power took care that the accusation should be supported by their testimony. The wretched man was seized, his property confiscated, and after languishing years in a dungeon he was at length turned out, penniless and blind, upon a world where he had not a friend to receive him. Then, in the very depths of his wretchedness, the Christians found him, even as their Master when on earth had found and received to his tender heart many a miserable sinner. From them he learned that his daughter was still living, and he had come to seek her, as soon as he had strength to travel, that he might entreat her forgiveness and then die.

"No, not die," said Paulina softly; "let me love you a little first."

He did not die but lived for several years in the pastor's family, reverencing the pastor's every word, caressing the little ones that came to the house, but clinging most of all to his long-lost daughter. He could not bear to have her absent, and if in the course of her duties she had to leave him for a little while, he sat listening for her returning

14*

footstep, which he was always the first to hear.

He received with gladness the doctrines of the gospel from the lips of the pastor, and words of comfort from his wife, but he could not seem to realize and appropriate to himself the hope they offered until at the last, just as the hand of death was sealing his lips forever, and he lay on his daughter's shoulder, gasping away the life he had so abused and wasted, he uttered these words:

"Forgiveness and peace."

They were satisfied. They believed that in the courts of heaven there was great rejoicing over this "brand plucked from the burning." "Though your sins be as scarlet," saith the prophet, "they shall become white as snow."

Encouraged by this wonderful mercy, Philip longed to hear good tidings from his own beloved parents, but they never came. Of Eudora he heard that she had married a wealthy Athenian, but no further. This informant was an Ephesian, travelling with dispatches to a Grecian legion in Gaul. " Had Tithonius no sons ? " he inquired of the messenger.

" He had one, but he died in Rome," was the reply ; and Philip knew that to all those who were bone of his bone and flesh of his flesh, he was indeed dead forever.

The traveller went on his way, little thinking how his words had torn open afresh the wounds of the Swiss pastor. The sickness of the body may be healed by physicians, or, if they fail, and the dear, frail tabernacle be entirely dissolved, yet we know that there awaits the freed spirit a mansion incorruptible in the heavens, whither we too may ascend ; but when the dearer *soul* is sick unto death, and the only physician that can heal is driven away, and there is nothing to look forward to but a hopeless eternity of separation—then love is torture and tenderness despair.

From friends in Rome they learned of Maximus. He had been very near the kingdom of heaven that night when he had followed the body of the young Christian martyr to its resting-place in the Catacombs. The Spirit was striving with him, the great truths whose power he had witnessed, and which his awakened conscience would not permit him to disbelieve, haunted him with their majestic beauty and sublimity; the way of life was opened to him, and he saw that its termination was the skies. But, alas! if the Spirit strove with him, he strove against the Spirit; truth stood before him, and he closed his eyes to it; the two ways lay open before him, and he deliberately chose that which led away from God and eternal life. The taunting words and mocking laugh of his companions were more to him than God's wrath; the pleasures and luxuries of his daily life more than the joys of a heaven to be purchased by self-denial. He was taken at his word. The Spirit ceased to strive, and he was apparently the same gay, joyous, careless man that he had been before his visitation. There were moments when time hung heavily on his hands as it had not done before, but he turned to the gambling table and played it away with dice. There were thoughts which would intrude upon his gayest hours, vague memories of a something better which had once been within his grasp, but he drowned them in the wine-cup. Pleasure seemed to have lost somewhat of its former power to charm, but vice held out to him her enticing hand and he grasped it; debauchery enticed him and he followed it; and so the end came, as it always must come sooner or later; always too soon to those who have left it entirely out of their thoughts and plans. There was a chariot race in the Via Sacra. The young nobles, flushed with wine, drove their steeds in headlong course along the Sacred Way. Two of them were drawing near the goal; already it was in sight; with many an oath and blow the maddened steeds were urged to their highest speed. There was a crash—a shriek—a confused medley of struggling horses and broken wood, and the bleeding, dusty *thing* that the bystanders dragged from under those iron hoofs and splintered wheels was only the shattered habitation of what might have been a noble soul. Its owner had departed. Whither? "As the tree falleth so it must lie."

Years passed. To the pastor of the Alpine valley they brought few changes save gray hairs and the bending of what had once been a stalwart form, only as he advanced in years his heart became more and more like the heart of a little child. He loved his work, he loved the people before whom he had gone in and out for more than forty years, he loved the mountains and valleys that surrounded his peaceful home, he loved the dear ones that filled that home with joy and thanksgiving; the old wife, fair and sweet as in her girlhood, her manly sons and rosy daughters, who watched with such tender affection her declining years, and the children's children that clustered in ever-increasing numbers around his knees,—and so it happened that when he heard the voice of men calling him to come up higher, he would fain have hid himself among the household stuff. But greater in soul and spirit than his generation, he could not be hid, and when he found it was the will of God, he submitted. In the councils of the Church he fought the battles of truth against error with a lion's strength and a lamb's gentleness, with the wisdom of the serpent and the harmlessness of the dove. In his wide bishopric he ruled as he had ruled his village flock—by the spirit of meekness and love. By his powerful intellect, by his brilliant, glowing eloquence, by his wonderful mastery over the minds of men, as well as by the saintliness of his daily life, he was the greatest man of his age, but in his perfect humility he lived his holy life and died his peaceful death utterly unconscious of that greatness.

Years passed. Over the drooping Roman Eagle towered the conquering Cross. Emperors bowed to it, kings acknowledged it, armies hailed it. Despotism, despairing to overcome it, changed its tactics, and clasping it to its breast, took it as a shield and banner. Then the refuge of the persecuted Christians, the burial-place of thousands of martyrs, became the mine from which Papal Rome drew its choicest treasures. In the Museum of the Vatican is a hall furnished entirely with relics from the Catacombs. There is nothing very attractive in their appearance. There are stone chairs and altars, oddly-shaped bottles and lamps, some of coarse earthenware, some of bronze, rude paintings, and still ruder carvings on slabs of clay or marble, broken and defaced and time-worn. These were once the coverings to tombs, which having been curiously opened, revealed nothing but a little dust to testify of their former occupant. On one of them, with the date line effaced, may still be read,

> Marcella of Rome,
> The fearless Christian Maiden,
> Martyred at the age of 21 years.
> She sleeps in peace, in the Lord,
> She will awake in the morning !

CHRONICLES OF THE SCHONBERG-COTTA FAMILY. 1 vol., 12mo $1 50

Fine edition. Crown 8vo, tinted paper 2 00
Cabinet edition, 16mo, tinted paper 1 50
Sunday-school edition, 18mo, illustrated . . . 1 00

Those familiar with the life of Luther will remember Dame Ursula Cotta, in Eisenach, who, when he was a lad singing from door to door to support him at school, took him to her house and ever after befriended him. The author of this book, for the purpose of reproducing in a more familiar form the social life, the religion, and some of the chief historical events and personages of that momentous period, finds in the above fact a suggestion on which to improve. The authoress manages her ingenious plot in the most skilful manner. One can scarcely persuade himself that these are not genuine documents fished out of some old Lutheran family chest

" It is intensely interesting, and will be a great favorite with the public. It is eminently one of the star books of the season."—*S. S. Times.*

" A book of unusual attraction and merit, where the interest never flags, and every page is full of gems. The work might justly be termed ' A Romance of the Reformation.' The various incidents in the life of Luther are portrayed with a graphic beauty and truthfulness rarely equalled." * * *

" It is seldom a book appears which, like this, has attractions for all classes of readers. The lovers of fiction and the lovers of history, the practical and the sentimental, the youthful, and those more advanced, are charmed by it, and its gentle catholic spirit will render it equally attractive to the Protestant and Romanist."—*Albany Times.*

" In this work we seem almost to meet the great men of the Reformation face to face, and to be actually present in the thrilling scenes in which they participated."—*Methodist.*

" The family history which it contains, if read by itself, would be regarded as one of the most successful portraitures of domestic life that has ever been drawn, each character being delineated and preserved with striking distinctness, and some of the characters being such as the reader will love to linger over as he would over some beautiful portrait drawn by a master's pencil."—*New York Observer.*

" The story from first to last is remarkable for its artlessness and tenderness, and it chains the reader's attention to the close."—*Am. Theo. Review.*

" The prominent scenes, from the time of Huss to the death of Luther, are painted before us, and we read them with such interest as even D'Aubigné can scarcely create. The book has all the fascination of a romance."—*Evangelical Repository.*

By the Author of "The Schonberg-Cotta Family."

THE EARLY DAWN; OR, SKETCHES OF CHRISTIAN LIFE IN ENGLAND IN THE OLDEN TIME. By the author of the Schönberg-Cotta Family. With Introduction by Prof. H. B. SMITH, D.D. 12mo $1 50
Fine edition. Crown 8vo, tinted paper 2 00
Cabinet edition, 16 mo, tinted paper 1 50
Sunday-school edition, 18 mo, illustrated . . . 1 00

The *Christian Life of England in the Olden Time* is here depicted, through several centuries, from its earliest dawn, in its contrasted lights and shadows, down to "the morning star of the Reformation." The Druid is first introduced in converse with the Jew and the Christian. The Two Martyrs of Verulam fall within the period of the Roman domination, full fifteen hundred years ago. The fortunes of an Anglo-Saxon Family are briefly sketched through three generations. The contests of the Saxon and the Norman, and their different traits, are vividly portrayed, in the time of the Crusades. And few tales are more interesting and instructive than that in which Cuthbert narrates his experience in the Order of St. Francis and his illumination by the "Everlasting Gospel" of Joachim, and Cicely relates how Dr. Wycliffe, of Oxford, ministered to her spiritual needs and insight.

"The undeniable charm of these sketches consists in their simple, truthful adherence to the spirit and traits of these olden times. The author has been a diligent student of the literature, and through the literature, of the very life of the epoch. This is revealed in many skilful touches of art, in incidental allusions, apt citations, and graphic descriptions of scenes and persons. But more than this is her rare gift of tracing the workings of the human soul in its needs and aspirations, its human love, its divine longings. The permanent religious wants, which remain the same under all varieties of external fortune, are so truthfully set forth that the Past becomes a mirror for the Present."—*Dr. Smith's Introduction.*

"The various facts and legends of Christianity are told in this book in a style of romantic fascination. It is an unusually entertaining and readable work."—*New York Evening Post.*

"The author carries us back into the midst of events and scenes, wakes up the dead actors and makes them live again, and we see not the history, but the living men that made the history."—*Evangelical Repository.*

"We do not know where to look for a book that combines such beauty of style, such charming simplicity and variety of expression, with such sweetness of spirit. It is full of beauty, and everywhere pervaded with a loving, catholic spirit."—*Hartford Press.*

By the Author of "The Schonberg-Cotta Family."

DIARY OF MRS. KITTY TREVYLYAN. A STORY OF THE TIMES OF WHITEFIELD AND THE WESLEYS By the author of the Schönberg-Cotta Family. With a Preface by the author for our edition. 12mo . $1 50
Fine edition, crown 8vo, tinted paper 2 00
Cabinet edition, 16mo, tinted paper 1 50
Sunday-school edition, 18mo, illustrated .   . . 1 00

The diary begins in 1745 and gives us a charming picture of rural life and simplicity in Cornwall. At the date the story opens the "mischievous fanatics," Whitefield and Wesley, begin to disturb the parish with their plain preaching. Kitty very soon goes up to London to pay a visit to the family of her uncle, who is a dissenter, and there she meets those reformers, who are turning the kingdom upside down with their new doctrines. The main interest of the book is religious, yet the state of the country at that time, the habits of society, the dangers of travelling, and the faithful pictures of the dress and manners of that age will interest all who are not attracted by the graver matters of the story.

"Notwithstanding the immense popularity of the Schönberg Cotta Chronicle, we should not be surprised if Mrs. Kitty Trevylyan completely rivals them in popular favor. All the good qualities that gained so much success for the writer's previous books are found in this, while the subject undoubtedly offers superior advantages to those where the scene is laid in remote times or in a foreign land. The family group in the old homestead, on the storm-vexed shores of Cornwall, becomes, from the author's skilful painting, and fine perception of character, a reality from henceforth to her readers ; and when the heroine leaves it to gain the glimpses of the great world that form the historical portion of the book, she carries with her the good wishes of all."—*N. Y. Times.*

"The beauty of the 'Diary' is its homelike simplicity, its delicate portraits, and powerful, because so perfectly natural, sketches of life and manners."—*Hartford Post.*

"The book is redolent with religious feeling, fresh, pure, and sensible ; it abounds in kind but keen thrusts at the follies and mistakes of conventional piety ; it pushes aside human creeds that fetter and conceal the Bible's plain, clear pages ; and it is quite remarkable for its nice detection of the starting-points of error, the places where divine doctrines have been spliced with human ones."—*Vermont Record.*

"We think this decidedly the author's best work, better even than the 'Cotta Family.' It sparkles on almost every page with gems of thought while the narrative is one of absorbing interest."—*S. S. Times.*

By the Author of "The Schonberg-Cotta Family."

WINIFRED BERTRAM; AND THE WORLD SHE LIVED IN. By the author of the Schönberg-Cotta Family. 1 vol. 12mo $1 75

Fine edition, crown 8vo, tinted paper 2 50

Cabinet edition, 16mo, tinted paper 1 75

Sunday-school edition, 18mo, illustrated 1 00

Unlike the author's previous works, it is not historical, but a story of modern life, with its scene laid in the heart of London. Winifred is a bright child, who very early in a naive way begins to be blasé, having nothing to do but gratify her own childish desires. The lesson of the book is that one can only live happily and profitably by sympathy with others, and in exertion to benefit others. The characters are all ordinary and natural people, and the plot is without one sensational incident, but the author's genius for irradiating the common, her simple, pure spirit, her delicate humor, her faculty of seizing upon and representing character with fidelity, and the lovely spirit of morality and religion, make the book a delightful one. The whole story is suffused with vivacity and grace.

"George Elliot, whom we regard as the greatest female novelist of the age, never exceeded the terseness and epigrammatic force of expression of some passages in Winifred Bertram. . . . . The allegory of the expanding and contracting chamber is one of the most exquisite things in modern literature."—*Round Table*.

"A charming and quickening story. as we might anticipate from the author."—*Congregationalist*.

"Delightful and charming are not properly descriptive of it, for while it is both, it is more than both; it is of the kind of books that one cannot read without growing better."—*Indianapolis State Journal*.

"It differs from its predecessors in that it is a story of our own time, but it is like them in its felicitous portraiture of character, its life-likeness in narrative and dialogue. and its exquisite illustrations of precious gospel truth."—*Christian Times*.

"In her previous works it might have been supposed that some part of their success was due to the happy choice of her subjects, or to the quaintness and novelty of the form in which they were presented. But here there is no gentle illusion of the kind, and the effect is to place her clearly foremost among the living writers of religious stories. It is altogether the best and ablest book of the accomplished author."—*Sunday-School Times*.

"A succession of pictures of conversations, scenes, and comments. which show a wonderful measure of shrewd common sense and genuine knowledge of human nature." -*National Baptist*.

By the Author of " The Schonberg-Cotta Family."

THE DRAYTONS AND THE DAVENANTS. A Story of the Civil Wars. By the author of the Schönberg-Cotta Family. 1 vol. 12mo $1 75

Cabinet edition, 16mo, tinted paper 1 75

Sunday-school edition, 18mo, illustrated 1 00

This work, the opening scene of which is in New England, is associated with a period of English history in the 17th century, involving political and religious questions in which Americans are deeply interested. In its vivid and truthful impersonations of character, its great historic interest, its inimitable pictures of domestic life, mingled throughout with an unaffected tone of religious sentiment, the author has fully equalled in this volume her Cotta Family, which has delighted so many thousands.

" On the whole, we are inclined to assign to this a higher position and greater merit than to any of Mrs. Charles' works."—*Independent.*

" If this work had preceded in its publication the Schönberg-Cotta Family, we are not sure that it would not have rivalled it in popular favor."—*New York Evangelist.*

" The quaint antique style of the volume gives it a strong flavor of those eventful times, while the tact and fidelity with which the prominent historical circumstances are interwoven with the fictitious incidents of the plot impart to it an air of naturalness hardly inferior to that of a cotemporary chronicle. With a curious instinct she seizes upon the heart of different epochs, incorporating it in her descriptions with equal faithfulness to the truth of history and of human nature."—*New York Tribune.*

" The volume starts with the first agitation of Protestantism as a political element in Great Britain, and proceeds through the civil wars that followed. The two families whose names afford a title to the volume were on opposite sides of the great question of the day, and the story is well wrought out in the well-known style of the author. Since the Schönberg-Cotta Family, Mrs. Charles has written no book which compares so favorably with the former as this."—*Methodist Protestant.*

" It is a living book, full of tender sympathies, holy thoughts, and devout quickeners, yet with sharp, clear-cut delineations of character. The roistering cavalier, the Christian reformer, and, more than all, the womanly women of the time, gather around us, and we know and love them."—*Christian Register.*

" To the descendants of the Puritans and those who respect their memory, this admirable volume will have a charm which even sympathy and interest rarely g've."—*New Haven Palladium.*

" All through the story there is evidence of that earnestness of feeling and refinement of thought that have given such a charm to this lady's writings, and have touched the popular heart so effectively while instructing and elevating the reader's tastes and moral and religious aspirations."—*Roxbury Journal.*

By the Author of " The Schonberg-Cotta Family. "

ON BOTH SIDES OF THE SEA. A STORY OF THE COMMONWEALTH AND RESTORATION. Being a Sequel to " The Draytons and the Davenants." By the author of The Schönberg-Cotta Family. 1 vol. 12mo . . . $1 75
　　Cabinet edition 1 75
　　Sunday-school edition, 18mo 1 00

While this work is complete in itself, yet its historical value and interest are very much heightened by reading it in connection with its companion volume, " The Draytons and the Davenants," where many of the leading characters are first placed before the reader. These two families are in this volume, as in the preceding, made the warp of the story, into which is woven the history of a most eventful period. Opening with the tragic scenes of the execution of Charles I., we have presented in the highly dramatic style of the author—the establishment of the Commonwealth under Cromwell, its brilliant career, the death of the Protector, the restoration of the Monarchy, and the forcible emigration to America of prominent actors in its previous overthrow.

" The house life, the public teaching, the political relations and partisanships of these times (1637 to 1691) are depicted with consummate power and impressiveness in this volume and the Draytons and the Davenants, to which it is a sequel."—*Brooklyn Gazette.*

" This work will be found to be a vivid reproduction of the scenes of those stirring days, which more than any other in profane history have an interest for *us*, and which all Americans need to understand."—*Christian Advocate.*

" The scenes of the period to which this volume refers are depicted with consummate skill and rare beauty, and with such perfect naturalness that the reader almost forgets that he is not in actual contact with the impressive realities."—*Albany Express.*

" It has all the varied interests and the peculiar charm which attach to the author's ideal and yet historic narratives that are now so familiar to the reading world. No writer of the present day has more deservedly won a place in the hearts of all who love the truth, and who can appreciate that which is pure in sentiment and in domestic life."—*New York Observer.*

" It blends history with romance, and interweaves most charmingly lessons of the richest moral instruction and the deepest experiences of the Christian life "—*National Baptist.*

" ' On Both Sides of the Sea ' has certainly a charming flavor of the quaint spirit of the time it describes, while as a story merely it is of exceeding interest."—*New York Mail.*

By the Author of "The Schonberg-Cotta Family."

MARY, THE HANDMAID OF THE LORD By the Author of the Schönberg-Cotta Family. 18mo, tinted paper. Cloth extra, red edges $1 00

This work is intensely devotional in its nature. The subject is Mary, the Mother of the Lord. Out of her life history the author has drawn a series of seven essays, all of which are pure as the water of life. The book is not historic, as are the other literary productions of the same lady, but its talent is none the less marked than that which is displayed in the Schönberg-Cotta Family. This fact is enough to recommend it to all lovers of truth and piety.

"It is written with all the accomplished author's charm of style, and breathes a devotion and fervor which cannot fail to kindle corresponding emotions in the heart of the reader "—*Christian Times.*

" Novelty of incident of course is not the charm of this beautiful book. It is the reverent and thoughtful tone of mind that the author brings to the contemplation of one of the most deeply interesting characters of holy writ."—*New York Times.*

POEMS. By the author of the Schönberg-Cotta Family. Comprising " The Women of the Gospels," " The Three Wakings," etc., with other Poems never before published. 1 elegant vol., 18mo. Cloth extra, red edges . . $1 00

The book is divided into three parts ; the first composed of a series of Poems on the Women of the Gospels (Mary the Mother of the Lord, Mary Magdalene, etc.) ; the second made up of miscellaneous pieces ; and the third comprising Hymns and Religious Poems.

"They are religious in character and earnest in expression, and will prove a very acceptable addition to our devotional books."—*Congregationalist.*

" The same clearness of expression, delicacy of sentiment, and purity of English, which mark her prose works, enrich these verses also."—*Southern Presbyterian.*

" We have not found in this collection a single poem which is not marked with some striking thought, while the correctness which is conspicuous in her prose compositions equally follows her through the mazes of her somewhat various verse."—*S. S. Times.*

" Some of them are very sweet, evincing not only much poetical talent but great devotional feeling."—*Ills. State Journal.*

Sovereigns of the Bible.

By E. P. Steel. With illuminated title and many illustrations. 16mo., beautifully bound, $1 50

The scattered facts in the Lives of the Kings of Israel and Judah are skilfully arranged in one continuous narrative, true to life as given in the Sacred Record, and useful to those who would gain a clear and continuous view of the Bible Kings and their times.

It is a valuable book for the Sunday School Library.—*S. S. Times.*

Elsie Dinsmore. By

Martha Farquharson, author of "Allan's Fault," etc. 16mo, illustrated $1 25

A beautiful and instructive story, in which the power of true piety in a very young child is admirably exhibited in a series of trials which, though severe and unusual, are not beyond the limits of probability.—*Am. Presbyterian.*

Elsie is environed with besetments and trials, but is singularly faithful through them all, and gives promise by her sweetness of character to be the means of saving others. The sequel of this story will be eagerly looked for, as it closes at a very interesting point in the narrative. It is a charming book, and will give increased popularity to the authoress.—*Phila. Home Journal.*

The Clifford Household.

By the author of "Independence True and False," etc. 16mo, illustrated 1 25

A tale illustrating the power of the religion of Christ in strengthening a gentle shrinking girl for the performance of difficult duties and the endurance of severe trials, and the power of the same religion in crushing and subduing a proud, imperious nature so that it bows at last to the rule of Christ. The story is well told.—*Presbyterian.*

The story is well told, and the spirit and lessons of the narrative are pure and evangelical.—*Am. Presbyterian.*

A lifelike picture of home scenes. No fancy sketch; no exaggeration; no perfect characters; no angels; but men, women, and children, as we find them in everyday life.—*Springfield Union*

The Finland Family; or

Fancies taken from Facts. A Tale of the Past for the Present. By Mrs. Susan Peyton Cornwell. 16mo, 3 illustrations. . $1 25

This excellent story has been so long out of print as to be new to the present generation of readers. "Its aim is to show the folly of a superstitious belief in signs and omens. It is full of the gentlest and sweetest sympathies, and at the same time commends the culture of the firmest and most steadfast principles."—*Chn. Intelligencer.*

Holidays at Roselands,

with some After Scenes in Elsie's Life. A Sequel to Elsie Dinsmore. By Martha Farquharson. 16mo, illustrated . . . $1 50

Elsie is here brought through various trials and a severe and nearly fatal sickness to full enjoyment of her father's affection, and the happiness of seeing him a humble follower of her Divine Master. The story is even more intensely interesting than in the first part, as with added years Elsie's character becomes more natural and mature. No reader of Elsie Dinsmore should fail to follow her story to its happy completion in this sequel.

The Brownings. A Tale

of the Great Rebellion. By J. G. Fuller. 1 vol. 16mo, illustrated 0 75

A deeply interesting story of the trials and sufferings of a Union family in the late war. The scene is laid on the banks of the St. Mary's, which separates Georgia from Florida. Impressive lessons, moral and religious, as well as patriotic, are conveyed through the medium of the story.

Lucy Lee, or All Things

for Christ. By J. G. Fuller 16mo, illustrated . . . 1 00

"This," says the *National Baptist* "is one of the few that we would like to have in every Sunday School library. It is written by one who knows the value of experimental religion, and to whom the service of God is a fountain of unceasing joy."

The two above volumes were formerly bound in one and called "The Brownings."

The Brewer's Family.

By Mrs. Ellis. A Temperance Story. 1 vol. 16mo . $1 25

We find this an admirable story of English life, by an English lady whose writings are well known on this side of the water. It describes how a Christian man, brought up to the business of a brewer, and until middle life never once imagining that there was in it any inconsistency with his Christian profession, was awakened at length to a sense of such inconsistency, and led to its abandonment. In his own experience in this regard his family also intimately shared. The story is an exceedingly interesting one, with an admirable lesson.—*Christian Times.*

The Kemptons. A Temperance Story.

By H. K. P., author of "Robert, the Cabin Boy," and other popular juvenile books. 16mo, 3 illustrations. 1 25

No better temperance book has been issued from the press for many years. It is a well-told story of youthful struggles and triumphs, beautifully illustrating the blessings of temperance, and showing the sad ravages of intemperance. Many of its passages are of thrilling interest, and its wide circulation would be of great service to the cause of temperance.—*Temperance Advocate.*

A capital temperance story. It differs from most of the stories on this subject in that the family who e history chiefly gives point to the argument is not that of a poor miserable outcast, but one of the highest respectability.—*Sunday School Times.*

Capt. Christie's Granddaughter.

16mo, 3 illustrations. 1 25

In our boyhood we loved to read books which brought tears to our eyes. This story of Captain Christie would certainly have held a high place in our list of favorites if tested by this effect. It is an English story of a retired sea-captain, living in Yorkshire with his grand-daughter and an orphan boy whom the old man adopted into his family; indeed, the interest of the story turns more on the boy than on the girl, but both are worthy of the love bestowed on them.—*National Baptist.*

The book is a valuable addition to our Sabbath School list.—*Sunday School Times.*

Amy Carr. By Caroline Cheesebro.

3 illustrations, 16mo. $1 15

A story of a girl who, when an infant, was left in the cars asleep, abandoned by its mother, and was taken home and adopted by the kind-hearted engineer. The girl becomes in the end a blessing to the house by bringing into it, after her own conversion, the benign influence of the gospel. The story is very interesting, many of the scenes being new to this class of books, and the teachings evangelical and good.—*Sunday School Times.*

Robert, the Cabin Boy.

By H. K. P., author of "Mary Alden," etc. Illustrated, 16mo. 1 15

A story of uncommon beauty and interest, about a boy who had been kidnapped when a child, and carried to sea by a sailor. The dangers and temptations of a sea life are forcibly depicted; also the great benefits of Bethel Societies and religious services for seamen, both when in port and when at sea.—*Sunday School Times.*

Jacques Bonneval; or, The Days of the Dragonnades.

A Tale of the Huguenots. By the author of "Mary Powell." 1 vol. 16mo 1 00

So lifelike are the scenes described, that one unhesitatingly lends his confidence, and follows the little company of martyrs through all their sufferings from Papal cruelty in France, until they are safely landed on the shores of England. The story is one of intense interest, with all the added charm of novelty, from its quaint language and careful correspondence with the historical events of the time.—*Hudson Co. Republican.*

Cherry and Violet. A Tale of the Great Plague.

By the author of "Mary Powell." 16mo, cheap edition . . 1 15

While not exclusively a religious tale, it is full of the spirit of self-sacrifice and dutiful affection, and expresses directly much true religious feeling.

This beautiful story of domestic affection, suffering, and self-sacrificing fidelity will be read by old and young with eager attention and pleasure.—*Christian Intelligencer.*

The Schonberg Cotta Books. 6 vols. 18mo, illustrated, in sets. (Any volume sold separately.) $6 00

"Young and old alike should read the entire set of Mrs. Charles' Works, if they would be refreshed in the purest waters of Christianity."

Chronicles of the Schonberg Cotta Family. 18mo $1 00

The times of Luther and the Reformation.

The Early Dawn.

18mo 1 00

Christianity in England from the earliest times to the days of Wickliffe.

Diary of Kitty Trevylyan. 18mo 1 00

The times of Whitefield and the Wesleys.

Winifred Bertram.

18mo $1 00

Modern English Life.

The Daytons and the Davenants. 18mo . . 1 00

The Civil Wars in Cromwell's times.

On Both Sides of the Sea. 18 mo $1 00

Continuation of the Daytons and Davenants, bringing the Puritans to New England.

For a fuller description of the Cotta Books, see our General Catalogue.

The Cousin Bessie Series. 6 vols. 16mo, beautifully bound in sets. (Any volume sold separately.) . . . $4 50

Cousin Bessie. A Story of Youthful Earnestness. 4 illustrations 0 85

A story of an orphan girl who was received into the family of her uncle, a wealthy merchant, where she made herself very useful to the worldly and ungodly family by her modest but steadfast no to every enticement to sin. The story is directed mainly against the drinking usages of society, and is a first-class temperance tale for people in fashionable life.—*S. S. Times.*

Tom Burton; or, The Better Way. 3 illustrations 0 85

The story of two journeymen mechanics, one of whom employed his leisure hours in reading and study, attending mechanics' institutes, etc. The other frequented the tavern. It is a good temperance story —*S. S. Times.*

The Grahams. By J. G. Fuller. Illustrated . 0 85

An officer in the United States army was killed at the storming of Chapultepec, in the Mexican war. This little volume tells the story of his widow and his three children; how the latter were educated, and

what became of each. There is a good deal of variety in the incidents, and the lessons inculcated are those of unselfishness and duty.—*S. S. Times.*

Toil and Trust; or, The Life Story of Patty, the Workhouse Girl. 3 illustrations 0 85

The life-story of a workhouse girl, showing that poor unfortunates of this kind are not always destitute of good elements in their nature, but may sometimes be moulded into usefulness and propriety. The volume contains also some powerful lessons on intemperance.—*S. S. Times.*

Alice and her Friends; or, The Crosses of Childhood. 3 illustrations 0 85

A book intended for the young especially, and showing that every child has a cross of some kind to take up. Mrs. Seymour, the wise woman of the book, first teaches her little daughter "Alice" what her cross is. Then, as her cousins and other friends visit her from time to time, the crosses of each are severally pointed out, and they are shown how to meet them. The story is arranged with much ability, and its teachings are as wise as they are impartial.—*S. S. Times.*

The Brownings. *For Description, see page 1.*

Alden's Stories for Young Americans. 4 vols.

18mo, illustrated, in sets. (Any volume sold separately.) . $2 00

Stories and Anecdotes

of the Puritans $0 50

As it is a kind of reading delightful to the young, and as the anecdotes give a just and exalted view of the Puritan character, we would commend the book to parents, as one of unusual value. It may be read by every one with great profit and interest.—*N. Y. Evangelist.*

The Example of Washington. With Portrait . 0 50

" A little volume of great value. The author does not pretend to give the example of Washington in his entire life, but employs the weight of his great name to arrest and fix the attention of the young upon some of the *essential* excellencies of character that were so fully illustrated in that unequalled specimen of human greatness; the prominent points in the work being the character of Washington as a religious man. The book should be in the hands of every youth in the land."

Fruits of the May Flower $0 50

The volume contains an accurate and somewhat full account of the origin of the Plymouth Colony, and of its progress during the first three years of its existence. The character and noble deeds of the Pilgrim Fathers are thus clearly brought to view. The facts stated are drawn from original documents.—*Preface.*

The Old Stone House;

Or, the Patriot's Fireside . 0 50

Under the guise of a familiar, pleasant tale of the Revolutionary era, Dr. Alden has here presented a condensed and most excellent compend of the elementary principles of the science of government, and our early political history. It strikes us as one of the most useful, as well as able and ingenious of the author's many juvenile works, and will be a good book for the family, and not less for the school-room.—*N. Y. Evangelist.*

The Fred. and Minnie Library. 5 vols. in

sets. (Any volume sold separately.) $3 75

Fred. Lawrence; or,

The World College. By Margaret E. Teller. Illustrated, 18mo 0 75

A deeply interesting story of an American youth devoting himself with a lofty sense of duty to the support of a dependent mother and sister, and gaining a strength and manly independence of character by the discipline he undergoes, as well as a cultivated mind. by a faithful and religious employment of his leisure hours. —*Am. Presbyterian.*

The Deaf Shoemaker,

and Other Stories. By Philip Barrett. Illustrated, 18mo 0 75

The author of this charming little book understands what will interest children, and how to adapt his style and language to their taste and wants. We cordially recommend it to a place in every Sabbath School and family library.—*Advocate and Guardian.*

Minnie Carlton. By

Mary Belle Bartlett. A beautiful story for girls. Illustrated, 18mo 0 80

The subject of this narrative is the eldest daughter of a household, forced by the death of her mother to take charge of it. The pledge given to her dying mother to train the little ones to meet her in heaven is conscientiously fulfilled, and the lessons of her example, prudence, and piety, rewarded by the most cheering results, bringing light and joy to the household, will scarcely be read without deep and grateful emotion.—*N. York Evangelist.*

The Russell Family.

By Anna Hastings. Illustrated, 18mo 0 75

A very beautiful and instructive story from real life, illustrating the power of a Christian mother, and the sweet influences of the domestic circle.—*New York Observer.*

Frank Forest. *For Description, see page* 6.

Charlotte Elizabeth's Works. 8 vols. 18mo,
illustrated, in sets $7 00

Charlotte Elizabeth's Works have become so universally known, and are so highly and deservedly appreciated in this country, that it has become almost superfluous to praise them. She thinks deeply and accurately, is a great analyst of the human heart, and withal clothes her ideas in most appropriate and eloquent language.—*Albany Argus.*

Separately as follows:

Judah's Lion . $0 85

Individuality of character is faithfully preserved, and every one is necessary to the plot. The reader will find in this book much information that he can only find elsewhere by very laborious research. Charlotte Elizabeth is a firm believer in the national restoration of the Jews to the possession of Palestine, but believes they will previously be converted to Christianity. We advise our friends not to take up this book until they can spare time for the perusal; because, if they commence, it will require much self-denial to lay it down until it is fairly read through.—*Christian Advocate and Journal.*

Count Raymond of Toulouse, and the Crusade against the Albigenses under Pope Innocent III. . . . . o 85

It is a striking, life-like picture of the sufferings of the Albigenses mingling the facts of history with sketches of personal character, and individual heroism, in a manner to excite an interest, and at the same time to instruct. It is a historical episode, replete with important lessons.— *New York Evangelist.*

Conformity, and Falsehood and Truth . . . . o 85

We read this little volume with great and unqualified satisfaction. We wish we could induce every professor of religion in our large cities, and indeed all who are in any way exposed to contact with the fashionable world, to read it. The author, in this little work, fully sustains her reputation as a very accomplished and superior writer, and the stanch advocate of Evangelical principles, carried out and made influential upon the whole life and conduct.— *Eng. Recorder.*

Judæa Capta . $0 85

'Judæa Capta,' the last offering from the pen of this gifted and popular writer, will be esteemed as one of her best works. It is a graphic narrative of the invasion of Judea by the Roman legions under Vespasian and Titus, presenting affecting views of the desolation of her towns and cities, by the ravages of iron-hearted, bloodthirsty soldiers, and of the terrible catastrophe witnessed in the destruction of Jerusalem. Her occasional strictures on the history of the apostate Josephus, who evidently wrote to please his imperial masters, appear to have been well merited.—*Christian Observer.*

The Deserter . o 85

The principal hero of the story is a young Irishman, who was led, through the influence of one of his comrades, to enlist in the British army, contrary to the earnest entreaties of his mother, and who went on from one step to another in the career of crime till he was finally shot as a deserter; though not till after he had practically embraced the Gospel. The account of the closing scene is one of the finest examples of pathetic description that we remember to have met with.—*Daily Citizen.*

Personal Recollections, with Explanatory Notes and a Memoir $0 85

We doubt if the lives of many females are blended with more incidents and richer lessons of instruction and wisdom, than the life of Charlotte Elizabeth. It will be found as captivating as any romance, and will leave on the mind a lasting impression for good.—*Albany Spectator.*

The Flower Garden.
o 85

A collection of deeply interesting sketches and tales, beautifully illustrated under the similitude of flowers.

DODD & MEAD'S

LATEST

JUVENILE AND SUNDAY-SCHOOL BOOKS,

762 BROADWAY, NEW YORK.

———

THE JUNO STORIES. A Series for Sunday-Schools. By JACOB ABBOTT. To be completed in 4 volumes. Beautifully illustrated and bound in fancy cloth, new style. Per volume $1 25

  1st. Juno and Georgie. In April.
  2d. Mary Osborn.   "
  3d. Juno on a Journey. In September.
  4th. Hubert.   "

Mr. Abbott, well known as one of the most successful writers of juvenile books in the country, has published nothing intended expressly for Sunday Schools in many years. This series, which is written in similar style to the famous Franconia Stories, is in the author's best vein, and will, it is believed, do its part toward meeting the urgent demand for a higher class of Sunday-school literature.

OLIVER WYNDHAM. A Historical Tale. By the Author of "Naomi." 16mo, fancy cloth, new style.
               1 50

An excellent and intensely interesting historical story by a well-known author. The scene is laid in the eventful period of the Great Plague and Fire in London, in 1665. A capital book for the older scholars.

THE OFFICER'S CHILDREN. A Story of the Indian Mutiny. By the Wife of an Officer. 18mo, illustrated, fancy cloth, new style. 0 75

A charming story founded on fact, and written by one who had a personal experience of the scenes described.

The story, while of intense interest, conveys incidentally a correct idea of Life in India at the time of the great mutiny.

THE SPANISH BARBER. A Tale of the Bible in Spain. By the Author of "Mary Powell" 16mo, illustrated $1 25

This beautiful tale will attract unusual attention from its subject as well as the reputation of its accomplished author. The story turns on the recent Revolution in Spain, opening the country to the Bible and religious toleration. Modern Spanish life is charmingly depicted, and the working of the recent changes strikingly illustrated in the varying fortunes of the Spanish Barber and his family.

"This little story is a narrative of the experience of a colporteur introducing the Bible in Spain at a period only a few years back. The author gives us no harrowing stories of the Inquisition, the rack, and the dungeon. The scene is laid principally at Gibraltar. It will be read with deep interest by those who watch the progress of Protestant Christianity."—*Chicago Commercial.*

PHILIP BRANTLEY'S LIFE WORK AND HOW He Found It. By M. E. M. 16mo, illustrated   1 15

"A story of the heart—simple, earnest, evangelical. It is written in the form of a daily diary, and recounts the experiences and struggles of a country boy who passed through college, on the way found Christ, and after sundry trials, which refined his Christian character, became pastor of a church in the Far West."—*S. S. Journal.*

"The account of the way Philip Brantley was led, and the way in which he at last found his life work, and comfort and happiness in it, will be read with interest, and will teach the youth who read it profitable lessons."—*Evan. Repository.*

UNCLE JOHN'S FLOWER GATHERERS. A Companion for the Woods and Fields. By JANE GAY FULLER. Beautifully illustrated with 9 engravings. 16mo, cloth extra 1 50

"This is an excellent book to put into the hands of children. It contains a great deal of information about the common flowers of our woods and fields, and connects this information with religious instruction in such a way as to leave a most happy impression of God's goodness on the young heart, and to cultivate at once a love of nature and a love of God. This book is rendered attractive both by an ingenious story and by numerous well-executed and tasteful illustrations."—*S. S. Times*

By the Author of "Mary Powell."

MAIDEN AND MARRIED LIFE OF MARY POWELL, *afterwards Mrs. Milton.* Printed in antique style, 16mo, tinted paper, cloth extra $1 75
   100 copies of the above have been printed in superior style on large paper, and can be had of the Publisher.

The story of Milton's courtship and marriage to Mary Powell, a country girl ; their estrangement and separation, which led to his famous treatise on divorce ; and her repenting and return to her husband, is told in this most charming of woman's diaries. Mary Powell still stands unequalled in this difficult field of authorship.

"This volume takes us back more than two hundred years, and sets us down in the midst of English society as it then was, and makes us live among its quaint scenes. It professes to be a diary of Mary Powell for a short time before her marriage with the great poet, and also for a brief period after that important event. Much that is valuable is produced in regard to manners and customs, and many interesting facts in the home-life of Milton are brought to light."—*Evangelical Repository.*

"In this delightful volume all is so natural, simple, and pleasant, that we linger over each incident with a strange unwillingness to leave it behind us. There is such a sweetness and grace in the way the young wife's tale is told, that one must read the book itself to get any fair idea of its winning beauty of expression."—*Southern Presbyterian Review.*

"Rarely have we met with a book so attractive in every way, investing with new interest the poet's story, and giving us a deeper insight into his life and character." - *Northwestern Presbyterian.*

THE HOUSEHOLD OF SIR THOMAS MORE. By the author of Mary Powell. New Edition, with an Appendix.
   1 vol., small 16mo, tinted paper, cloth extra . . . $1 00

The supposed writer of the beautiful diary is Margaret Roper, Sir Thomas More's favorite daughter. The charming picture of the High Chancellor's home-life abounds in allusions to other distinguished men of the time, and especially to Erasmus, the great scholar

By the Author of ' Mary Powell."

and reformer. The Appendix contains a sketch of the life of Eras
mus, and some interesting facts in Sir Thomas More's history with
notices of his interesting family.

" The story is remarkable for its beauty, sin.plicity, and pathos. The interest of
the reader is caught at once, and he only needs to read a few pages before he feels
himself a member of the family, listening to the delightful conversations of Sir Thomas
and the good Erasmus, smiling at the sweet simplicity of Meg's courtship, weeping
with her and all the family when the dark clouds of disaster commence to gather
about the household."—*N. Y. Evening Gazette.*

" Redolent of English air, herbage, and moral heroism, charmingly antique, and
in point of literary ability and execution equal, if not superior, to the previously pub.
lished productions, this volume deserves perusal as the record of a good. brave man
who in olden times, like his favorite Thames, upbore the weary, and gave drink to
the thirsty, and reflected heaven in his face."—*Christian Advocate.*

CHERRY AND VIOLET.   A TALE OF THE GREAT
PLAGUE. By the author of MARY POWELL. 1 vol.
16mo. Cloth extra, red edges $1 00

Cherry, who is supposed to write the history, lives with her father,
a hair-dresser on London Bridge. Her simple story brings in the historical events of the Plague, The Great Fire, and The Restoration of
Charles II. "These she describes with certain delicate touches
which only a woman can give," while the story of her life is told with
a beauty and artlessness which chain the reader's attention.

" It is not often that we read through a book at a sitting, yet when one has put
such a cup to his lips it is hard to lay it down till he has drawn the very last drop.
To speak soberly, Cherry and Violet is one of the most charming stories we have read
.n many a day. If all fictions were like this we could wish the number increased. It
is a simple picture of Life in London two hundred years ago."—*N. Y. Evangelist.*

" There is a charming quaintness in the style, and altogether the book is well fitted
to meet the expectations of those who remember the sweet historical romance of
Mary Powell. by the same gifted author."—*American Presbyterian.*

" This beautiful story of domestic affection, suffering, and self-sacrificing fidelity,
will be read by old and young with eager attention and pleasure."—*Christian Intelligencer.*

By the Author of "Mary Powell."

PASSAGES IN THE LIFE OF THE FAIRE GOS
PELLER, MISTRESS ANNE ASKEW, RECOUNTED
BY THE UNWORTHIE PEN OF NICHOLAS MOLDWARP, B.A.,
and now first set forth by the author of "MARY POWELL."
A new edition, 16mo, tinted paper, cloth extra . . $1 00

"The narrator represents himself as a governor or tutor in the house
of Sir William, to whom the fair Anne was devotedly attached, who
befriended her when her own kindred spurned her as a heretic, and
followed her to prison and the place of execution. The story of her
beautiful life, and sad, yet glorious death, is touchingly told. While
the details of the narrative are necessarily fictitious, it has the simple
charm and delightful freshness of veritable history."

"The character of Anne is most exquisitely drawn, and the events in her life are
so pathetically and naturally recounted, that it is scarcely possible that the book should
fail to charm its readers, whether Catholic or Protestant."—*Georgetown Courier.*

"The story of the Faire Gospeller, who was burned at the stake in London, in
1536, is very beautifully and touchingly told."—*N. Y. Citizen.*

"One is carried back in a wonderful way by its old style, form and manner, and
the recital of events as by one who witnessed and shared them, into the very midst
of the times when Anne Askew suffered so bravely in the cause of her Lord."—
Christian Times.

JACQUES BONNEVAL; OR, THE DAYS OF THE DRA-
GONNADES. By the author of Mary Powell. 1 vol.
16mo $1 00

"A young Huguenot is made to relate the story of the sufferings
and persecutions that resulted among the French Protestants from
the revocation of the Edict of Nantes. It is a beautiful story, told
with a simplicity which may well be supposed to have marked the
Huguenot character."

"So life-like are the scenes described, that one unhesitatingly lends his confidence,
and follows the little company of martyrs through all their sufferings from Papal
cruelty in France, until they are safely landed on the shores of England. The story
is one of intense interest, with all the added charm of novelty, from its quaint language and careful correspondence with the historical events of the time."—*Hudson
Co. Republican.*

"The pictures of heroism, suffering, and endurance are true to history, and drawn
with graphic power."—*Monthly Religious Magazine.*

MATRIMONY; OR, LOVE AFFAIRS IN OUR VILLAGE TWENTY YEARS AGO. By Mrs. CAUSTIC. 12mo. $1 50

" It is a lively, moving, truthful, affecting picture of life, as it will be found to exist in every village in this Christian land."—*Albany Spectator.*

" It is an *uncommonly* well written and impressive tale, designed and adapted to remedy certain great social evils, and to promote true social refinement."—*Puritan Recorder.*

" There are passages of the most thrilling truthfulness, and it is, as a whole, more captivating than one out of a thousand novels."—*Spectator.*

MACDONALD.—THE BOOK OF ECCLESIASTES EX-PLAINED, CRITICALLY AND POPULARLY. By JAMES M. MACDONALD, D.D., of Princeton, N. J. 12mo $1 75

The want so generally felt of a commentary on this portion of the Scriptures in a form accessible to all, and suited to the people as well as to scholars, is here supplied.

" This volume is devoted in the first place to an argument in proof of the position that immortality was revealed in the Hebrew Scriptures, and in the second place to the unfolding of the exact signification of the book of Ecclesiastes, for the benefit, rather, of the common reader, than the professed scholar. It contains a revised version, printed in parallel columns with the authorized version, and a brief comment on each verse. It will be found a useful help to Biblical study."—*Congregationalist.*

NEWCOMB.—THE YOUNG LADIES' GUIDE TO THE HARMONIOUS DEVELOPMENT OF CHARACTER. By HARVEY NEWCOMB. New and improved edition, 12mo, $1 50

" Mr. Newcomb has sought to present the best method of development of all the powers so as to produce the highest degree of cultivation, social, intellectual, moral, and religious."—*National Intelligencer.*

" It is written in an easy, unaffected manner. The subjects are well divided, clearly and logically discussed; every position of the author is proved from Scripture, and comes home with an irresistible power to the heart. It is in fact what might be technically termed a searching book, and as such is calculated to do much good." - *Brooklyn Athenæum.*

PULPIT ELOQUENCE (History and Repository of); *Deceased Divines;* containing the Masterpieces of Bossuet, Bourdaloue, Massillon, Fléchier, Isaac Barrow, Jeremy Taylor, Chalmers, Robert Hall, McLaurin, Christmas Evans, Edwards, John M. Mason, etc. With DIS-COURSES from the Fathers and the Reformers, and the marked men of all countries and times, from the Apostles to the present century; with Historical Sketches of Preaching in each of the countries represented, and Biographical and Critical Notices of the several Preachers and their Discourses. By HENRY C. FISH, D.D. A new edition. Two volumes in one, large 8vo. Cloth extra, . . $5 50

It is believed to contain a very complete *history of preaching,* and of the great *pulpit orators ;* and to embody an amount of *Christian eloquence,* on a great *variety of topics,* such as was never before presented in anything like the same compass. More than *eighty different preachers* are here represented ; each by a brief sketch, and by his *most celebrated discourse.* Under the Greek and Latin pulpit, there are eight discourses ; under the English, twenty-two ; under the German, ten ; under the French, eleven ; under the Scottish, nine ; under the American, sixteen ; under the Irish, four ; under the Welsh, three. It will be seen that *more than thirty are from foreign languages.* The *translations* are uniformly from high sources.

About fifty of these discourses are not accessible to the public except in this work, and most of the others are from works exceedingly rare and costly. The sermon of John Knox, for example, is the one for which he was arrested and forbidden to preach, and is the only extant discourse the great reformer put forth.

"The idea has been carried out with wonderful completeness. Such a body of homiletic literature, embracing so great a variety, and so instructive indications, has never been brought together before. . . . . The interest and value of such a collection can hardly be over-estimated."—*Evangelist.*

"The historical information communicated in these volumes will, of itself, more than repay the expense of their purchase."—*Bibliotheca Sacra.*

"The biographical and critical notices add much to the value of the work."—*Independent.*

"The work is a library in itself, which every theological student, clergyman, and layman will be proud to own."—*Public Ledger.*

"No clergyman who would possess an illustrated history of pulpit eloquence can dispense with this most stimulating and rewarding work."—*Congregationalist.*

PULPIT ELOQUENCE OF THE NINETEENTH CENTURY. Being supplementary to the History and Repository of Pulpit Eloquence (deceased divines) ; and containing Discourses of Eminent Living Ministers in Europe and America. Accompanied with Sketches Biographical and Descriptive. By HENRY C. FISH, D.D. With an Introductory Essay by Prof. EDWARDS A. PARK, D.D. One large volume, 8vo. Illustrated with seven large Portraits from steel. Cloth $4 00

Nearly sixty of the most distinguished Preachers of the present day are here introduced, about forty of whom belong to foreign countries. The Discourses have been almost uniformly prepared expressly for this work, or selected and designated by their authors themselves. They are, therefore, no ordinary productions ; but will be esteemed worthy, it is believed, of being placed with the " Masterpieces of Pulpit Eloquence " of other ages. The materials of the Biographical Sketches have in all cases been derived from responsible sources.

As indicative of the character of the work, it may be stated, that, under the German Pulpit, such men as Professors Tholuck, Julius Müller, Nitzsch, Drs. Krummacher and Hoffman, Court Preachers to the King of Prussia, will be found ; under the French Pulpit, Drs. J. H. Merle D'Aubigné, Gaussan, Malan, Grandpierre, and the celebrated Adolphe Monod (deceased since the preparation of the work was commenced) ; under the English, Melville, and Noel, and Bunting, and James, and the like ; and under the Scottish, Drs. Hamilton, Cummings, Buchanan, Guthrie, Duff, Candlish, and others.

The American Pulpit is represented by eminent men in each Evangelical denomination, selected with great care, and after wide consultation. Most of the Discourses in this department appear in print now for the first time.

" The biographical sketches are compiled with care, and, along with an outline of the history of each individual named, contain brief critical discussions of their merits as preachers and as divines. These criticisms are, so far as we can determine, just and discriminating. Altogether, this volume, like its predecessors, is a highly valuable and acceptable contribution to our religious literature, and will be an acquisition to the library of any reading man, whether he be a minister or layman " — *Christian Times.*